Also available in the Guys Read Library of Great Reading

GUYS READ

TRUE STORIES

EDITED AND WITH AN INTRODUCTION BY
JON SCIESZKA

STORIES BY

CANDACE FLEMING, DOUGLAS FLORIAN, NATHAN HALE, THANHHA LAI, SY MONTGOMERY, JIM MURPHY, T. EDWARD NICKENS, ELIZABETH PARTRIDGE, STEVE SHEINKIN, AND JAMES STURM

WITH ILLUSTRATIONS BY
BRIAN FLOCA

WALDEN POND PRESS
An Imprint of HarperCollinsPublishers

Walden Pond Press is an imprint of HarperCollins Publishers.
Walden Pond Press and the skipping stone logo are trademarks and registered
trademarks of Walden Media, LLC.

Library of Congress Cataloging-in-Publication Data
Guys read : true stories / edited and with an introduction by Jon Scieszka ; with
illustrations by Brian Floca. — First edition.
        pages   cm. — (Guys read ; 5)
      ISBN 978-0-06-196382-7 (hardback) — ISBN 978-0-06-196381-0 (paperback)
    1. American prose literature—21st century—Juvenile literature.   I. Scieszka,
Jon, editor.   II. Floca, Brian, illustrator.
PS659.2.G89   2014   2014010024
818'.609—dc23   CIP
                                                                       AC

Typography by Joel Tippie
16 17 18   PC/RRDH   10 9 8 7 6 5 4 3
❖
First Edition

CONTENTS

BEFORE WE BEGIN . . .

Have you ever imagined what it would be like to grow up in Vietnam during a war, to hunt for tarantulas in the Amazon, to learn how to play the guitar using a wire from an old broom, to almost die canoeing down a wild Alaskan river?

Ever wondered if you could draw comics, if you could learn science from reading poetry, if you could fix an aching tooth by pounding it into the roof of your mouth?

Can you guess what it was like to be the first person in America to see the largest elephant that ever lived, to be shipwrecked then captured and enslaved in the desert with nothing to drink but your own urine, to be left for dead in the Wild West and survive by cleaning out your wounds from a she-bear's claws by lying on a bed of maggots?

Well, imagine, wonder, and guess no more.

Because you'll find all of these things and more in this volume of the Guys Read Library of Great Reading, *Guys Read: True Stories.*

This is the beauty of a particular kind of writing called nonfiction or, lately, "informational text." But I like calling it nonfiction because that's exactly what it is—not fiction. It's not made-up. It's true.

Field & Stream editor T. Edward Nickens really did almost die canoeing down an Alaskan river.

In the 1730s a guy who went by the name of La Roche Operator traveled around the country pounding people's aching teeth into their mouths . . . and charging them for it.

Sy Montgomery hiked the Amazon, hunting for tarantulas.

Doug Florian has written a collection of real science— and real funny—poetry.

Candace Fleming knows that Jumbo the elephant brought in a total of $1.5 million in ticket sales in his first year in America . . . and released up to four hundred pounds of his "business" per day.

But don't thank me for adding all of this awesomeness

to your knowledge. Thank our curious and hardworking writers. And thank our artist, Brian Floca, a very talented nonfiction writer himself, for his wonderful illustrations for each story. And for his almost-historical cover.

These are some amazing stories.

Both true and truly worth checking out.

Jon Scieszka

SAHARA SHIPWRECK
BY STEVE SHEINKIN

Like many great survival stories, this one starts with a shipwreck. To be precise, it starts with the American brig *Commerce* slamming into a reef off the coast of West Africa on the moonless night of August 28, 1815.

The ship's side cracked wide open, and seawater poured in. The good news is Captain James Riley and his eleven-man crew loaded a lifeboat with barrels of water, bread, and salted meat and made it to shore. The bad news is they'd just wrecked on the western edge of the Sahara desert. Also unfortunate: Shortly after sunrise a band of spear-wielding bandits spotted the sailors, robbed them, and carried one off as a slave. Riley and his remaining crew escaped to sea in their rickety lifeboat. They had a few bottles of water, a few pieces of salt pork, a sack of soggy figs.

Seven days later they were still in the boat.

They'd hoped to spot a passing ship. No luck. The nails holding their vessel together were working loose in the waves, and the boat was coming apart beneath them. Their legs were underwater; their upper halves roasting in the sun. The food was gone. The water was gone. Abandoning hope of rescue, Riley and the men paddled to shore and collapsed on a patch of wet sand. Exhausted, starving, and utterly lost, the men moistened their burning throats with sips of their own urine.

It was at this point that the pleasant portion of their journey came to an end.

At dawn Riley stood on a narrow beach, looking up at a rocky cliff rising a hundred feet from the sand. A powerfully built man of thirty-seven, the captain stood over six feet tall and weighed 240 pounds (remember that number). He wondered what was above the cliff. He said a silent prayer that, in the past week, they'd drifted far enough south to get past the dreaded Sahara.

But first things first—the crew was desperate for food and water. Searching the beach, they found and devoured a few mussels, which did nothing for their hunger but did succeed in intensifying their thirst to the level of torture. Hoping to find edible plants on the land above the cliff, the men began walking along the beach, searching for a way up.

Many boulders, fallen from the cliff above, blocked their path. The men climbed over the smaller ones and waded through neck-high surf, clinging to one another, to get around the ones they couldn't climb. The sun's rays bore down from a blindingly bright sky.

Riley had now gone so long without freshwater, his saliva had stopped flowing. "My tongue," he would write, "cleaving to the roof of my mouth, was as useless as a dry stick." Only way to get it unstuck: a sip of urine.

After hiking all day, accomplishing nothing, the men lay down in their wet clothes. The captain gazed at the youngest member of his crew, the fifteen-year-old cabin boy, Horace Savage. Before setting out, Riley had promised Savage's mother that he'd watch over the boy as he would his own son. Now, even in sleep, Horace's face was twisted with pain and terror. "I took him in my arms," Riley wrote, "and we all slept soundly till morning."

At dawn, while the crew scooped holes in the sand in a frantic search for freshwater, Riley found a place where the cliff looked climbable and began a slow ascent. Dragging himself up and over the edge, he stood and gazed out to the east.

He fell to the ground in shock.

No trees. No grass. Nothing green in sight. Just rocks and reddish-tan sand straight to the horizon. "Despair now seized on me," the captain confessed, "and I resolved to cast myself into the sea as soon as I could reach it, and put an end to my life and miseries."

But he thought of his wife, Phoebe, back home in Connecticut. He thought of their five children. He thought of his ten men on the beach below. He started down the cliff.

The crew gathered around to hear the news. Riley warned it wasn't good, but there was nothing keeping them on the barren beach. They climbed the cliff and stared in horror at their new home. Many of the men began to weep.

"Nothing can live here," one said.

Another muttered, "Here we must breathe our last."

The *Commerce* men were standing on the western edge of the Sahara desert. Stretching three thousand miles across Africa, this is a desert about the size of the United States. Daytime temperatures soar to 120 degrees. After sunset, without moisture in the air to hold the heat, temperatures can plunge into the 30s.

Riley encouraged the men to move. He told them there'd be plenty of time to lie down and die when they could no longer walk. They trudged along on sand baked as hard as stone and hot enough, Riley thought, to fry eggs. By dark they were near collapse.

"I think I see a light!" cried one of the sailors.

In the distance was a campfire. "Joy thrilled through my veins," Riley recalled. "Hope again revived within me." The captain's "joy" shows just how desperate he was. According to stories he'd heard from fellow sailors, Christians marooned in the Sahara were seized and enslaved by the native nomadic tribes.

Well, at least they might get something to drink.

The next morning Riley prepared his crew for what lay ahead. "Submit to your fate like men," he told them. "We must submit to save our lives." If enslaved, the captain explained, the men's one hope would be to somehow convince their masters to take them north to a port city in Morocco. There, with luck, an American or European merchant might agree to buy them and set them free.

They walked toward a camp with dozens of white tents and a few hundred camels. A man in the camp spotted the approaching sailors. Drawing his scimitar and screeching, he ran toward the strangers. Within moments about forty men and women in flowing robes were sprinting toward Riley's crew, many waving guns and swords.

Riley and his men bowed to show submission. The nomads charged into the group of sailors, several grabbing for each American, fighting over which slave would belong to which family. Riley stood helpless as his captors began yanking off his clothes. The same was done to the other sailors. "We were all stripped naked to the skin," Riley said.

Now officially slaves, the men were marched back toward camp. Their new owners were members of a Bedouin tribe known as the Oulad Bou Sbaa, Arabic-speaking nomads who traveled the western Sahara by camel in a never-ending search for forage and water.

In camp the camels were gathered around a well, drinking from a trough. The sailors tried to wriggle their way to the water. Children laughed at the sight of these pale, naked men hopelessly shoving between the legs of the much stronger beasts. Adults joined the fun, shouting insults— the most popular was "Christian dogs."

Eventually an ancient woman set a bowl on the ground in front of Riley. He stuck his head in and downed half a gallon of warm, sandy water. Around the camp the other captives were guzzling as greedily. They knew better (a dehydrated body can't absorb water very quickly), but they couldn't stop themselves. Right away, the muddy liquid began squirting out the other end, streaming down their bare legs. The men didn't care. They kept drinking.

Their thirst temporarily slaked, the captives' hunger suddenly roared. The men begged for a bite to eat but were told there was absolutely no food in camp.

Later that morning the Bedouins packed up their tents and filled their goatskins with water. An ingenious adaptation to desert life, the goatskins were just that—an entire goat's skin, with the head, bones, and everything else carefully removed. The open neck was the spout, tied with rope to keep the water from spilling.

Once the camels were loaded, the masters ordered the animals to kneel, and made signs with their hands for the slaves to climb on behind the humps. The sailors swung their legs in the air and planted bare butts on bristly backbones. The unpleasant sensation was difficult to describe—not unlike, Riley guessed, sitting nude on the edge of an oar.

That's when the camels were standing still. As the caravan set out, the men clung to fistfuls of camel hair to keep from sliding off. "It seemed as if our bones would be dislocated at every step," the captain recalled. Meanwhile, the insides of the men's thighs were rubbed raw against the camels' swaying haunches. Some of the men purposely fell from their camels, preferring to walk. But they had to run to keep up, and the rocky ground sliced open their bare feet.

Also it was getting kind of hot. "Our skins," wrote Riley, "seemed actually to fry like meat before the fire."

The sun finally set and the air cooled, but still the Bedouins pushed on. "I cursed my fate aloud," Riley remembered of this moment. "I searched for a stone, intending if I could find a loose one sufficiently large, to knock out my own brains."

Just his luck, he couldn't find a loose stone.

The caravan stopped around midnight, having covered forty miles. The camels were milked, and women carried bowls of warm milk to the captives. Each was allowed to gulp about a pint. It tasted delicious but barely dented their hunger or thirst. As the men lay on the gravelly ground and attempted sleep, a chilly wind lifted clouds of sand and caked the jagged grains to their blistered skin. Riley listened to his crew groaning in misery through what he described as "one of the longest and most dismal nights ever passed by any human beings."

There would be many more just like it.

* * *

In the morning the captives stood up, stiff and shivering. Each was given a sip of camel's milk and then ordered to prepare the camels for another long march. "The situation of our feet," Riley wrote, "was horrible beyond description."

After another excruciating march, the slaves spent the night in a larger camp. Curious Bedouins came to have a look at the Americans, and Riley saw revulsion on their faces. "We were certainly disgusting objects, being naked and almost skinless."

The captain watched the Bedouins kneel on the sand and bow their bodies toward the east in prayer. They were devout Muslims, Riley realized. He listened as they recited prayers and passages from the Koran. Riley had an ear for languages and was able to begin recognizing some Arabic words.

Later many members of the tribe gathered around Riley and, using a combination of Arabic and hand gestures, asked him to tell the story of how he had wound up in Africa. Riley responded in Spanish, which one of the old men seemed to understand. After telling of the shipwreck, Riley told his listeners that if they would take him north to a trading port in Morocco, he could be sold there at a great profit.

The Bedouins shook their heads. Impossible. Too far to travel. No water for the camels along the way.

So Riley and the other captives returned to their agonizing routine: broiling all day, whimpering all night. The group camped where they found dry, thorny bushes for the camels to eat. They found no water. They found nothing edible for humans.

"The sun beat dreadfully hot upon my bare head and body," Riley wrote of these seemingly aimless wanderings. "It appeared to me that my head must soon split to pieces."

The other slaves were as bad off, or worse. The men's burned skin peeled off in sheets, and the raw, red layer beneath bubbled in the blazing sun. A crew member named James Clark, Riley noted, was "nearly without a skin." The captain was even more alarmed by the condition of another sailor, George Williams. "His skin had been burned off," Riley wrote, and "hung in strings of torn and chafed flesh. His whole body was so excessively inflamed and swelled, as well as his face, that I only knew him by his voice."

Riley continued to drink his own urine, though it turned dark orange as the fluids in his body dried up. At this extreme stage of dehydration, the body no longer produces tears or sweat. The eyes sink into their sockets. Muscles cramp and spasm, making movement awkward and painful.

At some point Riley realized he'd been sold from one family to another for a blanket. It hardly mattered.

Quietly cursing their captors as "savages" and "barbarians," the Americans continued moving southeast, usually about thirty miles a day. There was nothing in sight but more of the same flat, rocky land in all directions. The slaves hung on the backs of camels or staggered along beside on feet so cut up, Riley wrote, "We could scarcely refrain from crying out at every step." Riley was traded again. His new owner beat him with a cane when he couldn't keep up.

The thought of conversion to Islam crossed the captain's mind. Maybe he'd get better treatment. But to convert, he knew, he'd have to get circumcised. Didn't seem worth it.

At night Riley was put to work searching for sticks for the campfire. Then he would sit and watch the men pray. How could such devout men, he wondered, be so inhumane? How could they buy and sell and abuse their fellow human beings?

It didn't occur to him then—though it would upon reflection—that he came from a religious country that did the exact same thing.

By September 18 (Riley was keeping track of the calendar by slicing his leg with a thorn for each day) the goatskins of water were nearly empty. The slaves lived on one cup of camel's milk per day, and the camels' milk was starting to fail.

The Bedouins gathered for a meeting, and Riley was able to follow some of their conversation. They'd given up on finding water. They would return to the well by the sea, where the *Commerce* crew had been captured eight days before. Just the thought of covering that ground again, this time without water, nearly crushed what remained of Riley's spirit.

Nearly—but not quite.

During the next day's journey, the captain saw a camel begin to let loose a stream of urine. He lurched forward, caught the liquid in cupped hands, and drank. Bitter, he thought, but not salty. The other slaves did the same. But anytime they drank anything, their hunger became unbearable. Riley saw some of his crew chewing strips of their own peeling skin. "I was forced," he wrote, "to tie the arms of one of my men behind him, in order to prevent his gnawing his own flesh."

At night he watched two of his emaciated sailors lure a Bedouin child out of camp. One of the men lifted a stone to smash the boy's head. Riley jumped in their way. "They were so frantic with hunger as to insist on having one meal of his flesh, and then they said they would be willing to die," wrote Riley. "I convinced them that it would be more manly to die with hunger."

A couple horrible days later Riley was lying in his master's tent, barely able to move. He watched two strangers ride into camp on camels packed with goods. According to custom, guests were to be offered water. There was none. Using sticks and tent cloth, women from the camp built the visitors a shelter from the sun.

"Where do you come from?" they asked the men. "What goods have you got?"

The men sat in the shade, each holding a double-barreled musket, and told their story. They were merchants and brothers, Hamet and Seid. They had traveled from their homes far to the north. They had blankets and blue cloth to sell.

Riley picked up a bowl and crawled out of his tent. He approached Hamet, kneeled, and pointed to his white, filmy mouth.

"*El rais?*" asked Hamet—"The captain?" The women had mentioned that their slave was a former ship's captain.

Riley's tongue was so stiff, he could not speak. He nodded yes.

Hamet walked to his camel, opened a goatskin, and

filled Riley's bowl with clean water.

"Drink, captain," he said.

Riley drank. In his best Arabic, he said, "God bless you."

Hamet was about Riley's age. Like Riley, he had a wife and children at home, in Morocco, but spent most of his time on long trading voyages. His last trip across the Sahara, from his village to the city of Timbuktu twelve hundred miles to the southeast, had ended in catastrophe. After two years of sandstorms and starvation, he'd returned home poorer than when he'd left. Desperate to earn enough to feed his family, he set out into the desert with his last few bundles of cloth.

The day after arriving in the camp of Riley's masters, Hamet asked the captain to sit with him. He wanted to hear Riley's story. In hand signals and elementary Arabic, Riley told of the shipwreck and of the crew's miserable travels. He told Hamet of his love for his wife and children, including the cabin boy Horace Savage, who he described as his eldest son.

As Riley spoke, a tear slid down Hamet's cheek. He wiped it away, saying, "Men who have beards like me ought not to shed tears."

That tear, to Riley, was a spark of hope.

He asked Hamet to take him north and sell him in Morocco. Hamet was intrigued. It might be possible, he said, for them to get to the port town of Swearah. Riley jumped at this, blurting out an outrageous lie. He said he knew the consul (the foreign representative) in Swearah. The man was a friend of his!

Hamet asked how much the consul would pay for Riley.

"One hundred dollars."

"You are deceiving me," Hamet said.

Riley swore he wasn't.

"I will buy you then," Hamet said. "But remember, if you deceive me, I will cut your throat."

Riley agreed.

Hamet haggled with Riley's owner, eventually buying the slave for a piece of blue linen and a few ostrich feathers. Riley begged Hamet to purchase Horace too.

It was too far to Swearah, Hamet said. The boy wouldn't make it.

"Let me stay in his place," Riley pleaded. "Carry him up to Swearah. My friend will pay you and send him home to his mother. I could never face her without him."

Again, Hamet was moved. "You shall have your son, by Allah."

He traded for the cabin boy. Riley then followed Hamet

around camp, pestering the merchant to buy more of the enslaved sailors. Hamet pointed out the dangers—they had eight hundred miles to travel, and a bigger group would need more water and would be easier prey for bandits. Riley wouldn't stop begging. Finally, incredibly irritated with his slave, Hamet agreed to buy the four other Americans in camp. (The three other *Commerce* men were in other camps, far beyond Riley's help.)

The slaves cost Hamet almost everything he and his brother had. If he was unable to sell the Americans, he was ruined.

Before setting out, Hamet knew, the slaves needed at least one meal. At midnight he and Seid silently led one of their extra camels—an old, scrawny beast—out of camp and into a gully beyond view of the tents. Riley gathered sticks and dung for a fire. Seid slid his scimitar across the camel's neck, and Hamet caught the flowing blood in a copper kettle.

According to Bedouin custom, anyone who has food is obliged to share—it's the only way to stay alive in such a harsh environment. At this particular moment, though, the brothers and slaves were not in a sharing mood. They'd been hoping to conduct the slaughter without awakening anyone. But once the kettle of blood began bubbling on the fire, the meaty smell drifted into camp. Everyone started coming out to see what was going on.

Hoping to beat the crowd, Riley and the other captives stuck their hands into the blood, which had congealed to a kind of pudding, and scooped scalding blobs into their mouths. Meanwhile, people started hacking off bits of the camel. Some carried off hunks of meat while others threw the liver, lungs, and uncleaned intestines into the blood pot. Someone else cut open the animal's stomach, dipped out a handful of pulpy, green liquid, poured it into the pot, and stirred the stew with a stick.

Hamet and Seid felt themselves lucky to get a few bites of intestine. The slaves were happy with the blood.

After a short night's sleep, Riley awoke desperate for a drink. He looked over at the camel carcass and saw a teenage boy bent over the beast's open stomach, drinking. Riley pushed the kid out of the way and stuck his own head in. "The liquid was very thick," he recalled, and "its taste was exceedingly strong." But he wasn't complaining. "So true it is," he noted, "that hunger and thirst give a zest to everything."

Hamet and Seid cut up the bits of remaining meat (just fifteen pounds from the entire camel) and laid it out to dry in the sun. From the camel's hide, the brothers made sandals for the Americans. Hamet gave Riley a small knife—a sign that Hamet trusted Riley and was counting on him to help lead the group through the challenges ahead.

Then the eight men set out for Morocco, taking turns riding the brothers' four camels. The slaves all had beards by now, and shaggy hair. They'd been able to scrounge rags or scraps of goatskin, so no one was completely naked anymore, though Riley was still shirtless. When they were a ways out of camp, Hamet pulled a shirt out of his saddlebag. He told Riley he'd stolen it.

"Put it on," he said. "Your poor back needs a covering."

Riley kissed Hamet's hand and put on the shirt.

He and the other Americans had started out thinking of their captors as Muslim savages. The captors had called them Christian dogs. Now, between Riley and Hamet at least, those views were beginning to change.

"Good Riley," Hamet said, "you will see your children again, inshallah (Arabic for 'God willing')."

Over the next few days, the men finished off the last of the camel meat. Their dehydrated bodies no longer produced urine, so the camels' was the only available beverage. The captain was down to about 120 pounds. They traveled fifteen hours a day in a life-or-death race for water.

"The remaining flesh on our posteriors, and inside of our thighs and legs, was so beat, and literally pounded to pieces, that scarcely any remained on our bones," wrote Riley. The captives' pain, hunger, and thirst made sleep at night impossible. "I cannot imagine that the tortures of the rack can exceed those we experienced."

On what Riley figured was September 30, Hamet and Seid led the caravan into a narrow canyon. There was a well nearby, Hamet explained.

Riley saw nothing but rock and sand.

"Look down there!" Hamet shouted, pointing to a pile of boulders.

Riley peered between the rocks. It was too dark to see. But, as his eyes adjusted, he could make out what looked like a dark pool. Water? He stumbled around the boulders and found an opening, allowing him to reach a trickling spring.

"Riley, drink," Hamet said, "it is sweet."

Riley drank. They all drank. The camels drank astounding amounts—sixty gallons apiece, Riley guessed.

With goatskins full, they set out again, soon reaching an area of soft, sandy desert, a mercy for their feet. Several days later they met up with a group of nomads who gave them boiled mutton and bowls of milk mixed with water. "This was indeed sumptuous living," commented Riley, amazed by the generosity of people who had so little.

The men journeyed on into a region of sand dunes and swirling winds. They were out of meat again but still had the bones, which they pounded to powder and ate. In mid-October they entered a more populous region on the edge of the desert. The group hobbled up a winding path into what looked to Riley like hopelessly barren mountains. But as they turned a bend in the road, they were stopped short by a vision that looked to them like heaven. A green valley. Trees lining a clear stream. Cows and sheep feeding on grass.

The slaves raced into the valley and fell face-first into the stream. As they rested in the shade of date trees, Hamet brought the captives a hunk of honeycomb. They bit off huge chunks with the baby bees still inside. It was so good, they cried.

From there, loaded guns in hand, the brothers led the way north. They walked along hilly paths toward the Atlantic coast.

"Many robbers and bad men inhabit these parts," Hamet told Riley.

Sure enough, they were followed by lurking bandits with muskets and scimitars—clearly hoping one of the slaves would fall behind and make easy prey. But the group moved quickly and stuck together.

They continued up and down hills, passing small towns surrounded by walls of rock and mud. They passed villagers working in gardens, travelers on horseback, women carrying firewood and jars of water. Standing on a cliff high above the sea, Hamet pointed to a barely visible spot along the coast, far to the north.

"There is Swearah, Riley."

"How far?"

"Ten days," said Hamet, "at our slow pace."

Hamet had a better idea. They stopped at a walled village, and Hamet announced he would hurry ahead to Swearah alone. Seid would stay and guard the slaves. It was time, he told Riley, to write a letter to his friend in Swearah.

"I have fought for you," Hamet reminded the captain, "have suffered hunger, thirst, and fatigue, to restore you to your family, for I believe Allah is with you. I have paid all my money on your word alone." He reminded the captain of their deal. "If your friend will fulfill your engagements and pay the money for you and your men, you shall be free.

If not, you must die for having deceived me. Your men will be sold for what they will bring.

"Get some sleep," Hamet said. "In the morning, you will write the letter."

Riley lay awake all night. His bold-faced lie had gotten them out of the desert—but what the @#%& was he supposed to do now? "To whom should I write?" he wondered. "I know nobody at Swearah."

The next morning Hamet handed Riley a scrap of paper, a reed, and some black ink.

"Come, Riley," he said. "Write."

With Hamet hovering over his shoulder, Riley dipped the reed in the ink.

"Sir," he began, with no idea who he was addressing (luckily, Hamet could not read English).

"The brig *Commerce*," Riley wrote, "was wrecked on Cape Bojador, on the 28th August last; myself and four of my crew are here nearly naked in barbarian slavery: I conjure you by all the ties that bind man to man, by those kindred blood, and everything you must hold dear, and by as much as liberty is dearer than life, to advance the money required for our redemption."

Riley promised the money would be repaid.

"Should you not relieve me, my life must instantly

pay the forfeit. I leave a wife and five helpless children to deplore my death. My present master, Sidi (a term of respect) Hamet, will hand you this, and tell you where we are—he is a worthy man."

Riley signed his name, folded the paper, and hesitated over how to address it. Finally he wrote: "English, French, Spanish, or American consuls, or any Christian merchants in Mogadore or Swearah."

Hamet set off with the letter. It would take him at least three days to get to Swearah, and as long for news to return. Riley and his crew could do nothing but wait.

During the day the captives were penned in a yard with cows and sheep. At night Seid locked them in a cellar and slept outside with a loaded gun.

Their sunburns began to heal. There was plenty of water and barley bread twice a day. It was delicious, but more than their shrunken intestines could handle.

"Our bowels seemed to ferment like beer," Riley noted.

A small price to pay.

The real torture was the waiting. Five days passed with no news, then six. On the seventh day, a traveler came into town and announced he had seen Hamet several days before, very near Swearah.

From that moment on, Riley nearly fainted every time the village gate opened. "I longed to know my fate," he explained, "and yet, I must own, I trembled at the thought of what it might be."

On the eighth night since Hamet had left, someone knocked at the village gate. Seid went to see who it was. The captives, sitting on the ground and shaking from a mixture of cold and fear, watched him return with a tall, well-dressed man.

The stranger walked into the yard. He looked the captives over, and his gaze rested on Riley. He took a step forward and uttered, in English, an all-time classic line:

"How de-do, captain?"

Riley felt his heart leap into his throat. He couldn't breathe. He jumped up. All the slaves did.

The stranger was holding out his hand. Riley grabbed it. He begged to know the news from Swearah.

"Habla español?" the man asked, switching to a language he actually knew.

Riley nodded.

The man introduced himself as Rais bel Cossim, close friend of Mr. William Wilshire, the English consul in Swearah. Hamet had delivered the letter to Wilshire. And here was Wilshire's response.

Riley took the paper with trembling hands. He was quaking too violently to read the words. He handed the letter to one of his crew members, then fell to the ground and listened as the man read aloud:

MY DEAR AND AFFLICTED SIR,
I have this moment received your two notes by Sidi Hamet, the contents of which, I hope, you will be perfectly assured have called forth my most sincere pity for your sufferings and those of your companions.

The letter got even better.

"I have agreed to pay the sum of nine hundred and twenty dollars to Sidi Hamet on your safe arrival in this town with your fellow sufferers," Wilshire continued. "You will be at liberty to commence your journey for this town on receipt of this letter."

Tears streamed down the captives' bony, bearded cheeks. They were going to make it home.

Curious people lined the road to watch the captives march into Swearah. The Americans washed and shaved and ate. Captain Riley asked for a scale. He weighed ninety pounds.

After a few weeks of rest, the Americans sailed home.

Back in the States, Riley wrote a book about his adventures. It was a huge bestseller. A teenager in Indiana named Abraham Lincoln loved the book, and it may well have influenced his view of slavery. Riley certainly thought differently about slavery than he had before. "I have now learned to look with compassion on my enslaved and oppressed fellow creatures," he declared, referring to the 1.5 million people held in slavery in the United States. "My future life shall be devoted to their cause."

Of the six men left behind in the Sahara, two made it home; the other four were never heard from again. One of the survivors, William Porter, later told his story to Riley. He'd been purchased by a Muslim trader who was determined to bring him north to Swearah. They were attacked by bandits. The trader was murdered. Porter changed hands a few times but eventually made it to a coastal town, and from there, to America.

Porter described the trader who had died trying to bring him to freedom. Riley was absolutely convinced it had been his friend Hamet.

Bibliography

King, Dean. *Skeletons on the Zahara: A True Story of Survival.* New York: Little, Brown and Company, 2004.

Ratcliff, Donald J. "Captain James Riley and Antislavery Sentiment in Ohio, 1819–1824." *Ohio History* 81 (1972): 76–94.

Riley, James. *An Authentic Narrative of the Loss of the American Brig* Commerce. Hartford, CT: Published by the Author, 1817.

Robbins, Archibald. *A Journal, Comprising an Account of the Loss of the Brig* Commerce. Hartford, CT: Silas Andrus, 1818.

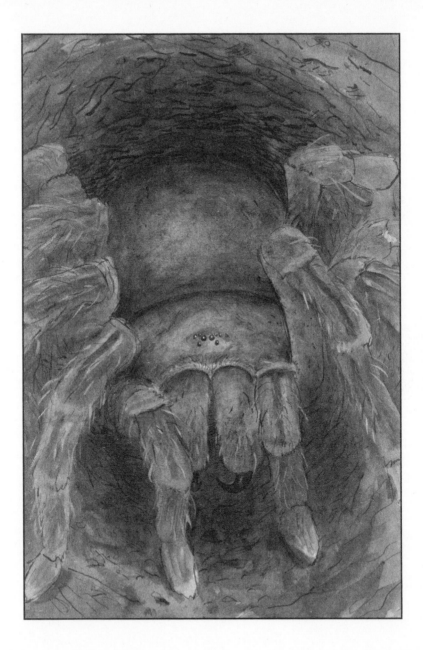

TARANTULA HEAVEN
BY SY MONTGOMERY

Here are some sounds you do not want to hear in the jungle: the sound of crumpling paper. (In the Amazon this usually means carnivorous ants are pouring from a tree.) The sound of cracking bark. (In Borneo it's a clue an orangutan is trying to push a tree down on top of you.) And neither do you want to hear a shout from a man who studies tarantulas for a living—a man who is not easily disturbed, a man who is only fifty yards away, but you can't see him for the jungle—uttering, with great distress and alarm, an unprintable expletive. Particularly when it is followed by the thud of 230 pounds of spider specialist hitting the ground and then crashing down a slope.

The week before Thanksgiving, we were somewhere

off-trail at the Trésor Reserve, our second day in the rain forest of French Guiana. With photographer Nic Bishop, I was researching a book to be titled *The Tarantula Scientist*, on the work of then-Ohio-based arachnologist Sam Marshall—whose distressed exclamation had just reached our ears.

"Sam?" I called. "Are you all right?"

Silence.

The day before, Sam had been telling us this forest was more benign than the beech-maple forest of Ohio. "There are fewer mosquitoes, no poison ivy, and as far as fer-de-lance"—that's the most common snake here, a species whose bite likely won't kill you but would require multiple skin grafts to fix—"I may have stepped over five hundred of them, but I never see any."

Maybe he had found one at last.

Seconds passed. Then, matter-of-factly, Sam spoke again: "I found a wasps' nest."

He'd found it by smacking his head into it. The nest was at face height, about six inches long, and looked exactly like the dead leaf to which it was attached. About 150 unhappy, black, half-inch-long wasps were swarming around it.

You might think Sam would keep an eye out for wasps, if for no reason other than self-preservation. There are the half-inch-long, solitary wasps that like to sip your sweat, which you notice when you lower your arm and the one in your armpit stings you. Then there are the huge, horrible, black *Pepsis* wasps, as big as hummingbirds. These slow-flying monsters attack tarantulas, paralyze them with their stings, and lay eggs in the still-living spider. Their larvae hatch and eat the spider's flesh. And then, there are more . . . but Sam really paid them no heed. "I was so focused on *Theraphosa*, I didn't see anything else," he explained.

You can get that way when you're searching for giant spiders—especially when the species in question is as magnificent, as surprising and mysterious, as the Goliath bird-eating spider, *Theraphosa blondi*.

This is the largest spider on earth. It can weigh three times as much as a mouse. (Think of a Quarter Pounder without the bun, but with hairy legs that could cover your face.) Such a creature deserves widespread fame, and yet so little is known about it that, despite its name, no one even knows what it eats. Although in one of its earliest scientific descriptions the spider was depicted eating a songbird, no one knows if the Goliath actually killed it or whether the bird just dropped dead and the spider scavenged it. Only twice have scientists ever seen *Theraphosa blondi* kill and eat anything in the wild: Once it was a worm, and another time a primitive amphibian-like creature called a caecilian.

No one knows how long *Theraphosa* lives (although some of the more than 800 species of tarantulas can live for thirty years). No one even knows if this largest of all spiders, so often sold embedded in Lucite as curios, is endangered by the practice—or endangered at all. Its populations might be thriving, or crashing.

It's important that people find out. And it's important that people care. These were among the many reasons I was there in French Guiana, researching this book for kids, the best readers in the world—and animals' bravest champions.

My other reasons? Sam's science was cutting-edge, and the work was thrilling. (Some might say too thrilling. "Why don't you write about kittens?" one of my mother's friends, shopping for a book for her granddaughter, asked me.)

Few of my friends understood why I would want to spend a couple of weeks purposely seeking large, hairy spiders. But going into this trip, I had had only one fear, and it was in direct opposition to the sentiments most people commonly express about such a venture: I was worried that we wouldn't find tarantulas.

* * *

Up until Sam's wasp encounter, our day had been going quite well. We were in Borneo at just the right time: Mid-November is the end of the dry season in this tropical country. "The spiders are more active now," Sam said. The forest around us was as hot as breath, alive with the songs of frogs and the calls of birds. The most auspicious sound to Sam's ears was the three-toned, off-key wolf whistle of the Screaming Piha—a creature whose calls occur so close to the emergence of the spiders that Sam calls it the *Theraphosa* Bird.

Sam had given Nic and me a simple chore: "Let's divide and search for holes with big, hairy legs." There were plenty of holes to search. Everything makes holes in this red, shallow, bauxite-studded soil: armadillos, toads, wasps, lizards, tortoises, snakes, possums. But the holes of *Theraphosa* are unmistakable, usually located beneath a branch, a root, or a stone. The ovoid entryway looks like the mouth of a little cave and sports a welcome mat of spun silk. "They're regular little Martha Stewarts," Sam said to us.

"It's best to hunt them going uphill, because the holes are pointing up at you," Sam said. "If you slip downhill," he advised sensibly, "you'll eventually crash into a tree and stop." This was good, because the slopes were quite steep, often more than 45 degrees, and the ground was covered with giant, wet leaves; rotting logs that give way under you; and the ankle-twisting holes of armadillos. But rolling and crashing into some of the trees here would be unwelcome. One of the palms here, as well as one of the vines, is covered with sharp spikes. And any wound in the tropics gets instantly infected.

Before long, though, and without spilling any blood, we had located our first burrow—"the entrance to the underworld," Sam called it—and then another. Sam showed us how to lure a tarantula out of its hole by wiggling a "Twizzle" stick in the burrow. Normally tarantulas spend the day in their silk-lined retreats, waiting until night to emerge. But of course tarantulas are ready to seize a good opportunity. In this case, she grabs the stick with her pedipalps, the pair of food-handling legs at the front of the head, and thunders out of her hole—her eight walking feet, each tipped with two hooflike claws, or tarsi, pattering loudly on the leaves of the forest floor. The sight of her takes our breath away. She is not even full-grown, but her head is the size of a fifty-cent piece. Her abdomen is as big as a quarter. She is covered with rich, reddish-brown hairs. Even immobile, she is very animate, alive with senses we can only dream of. Though her eight eyes are nearly blind, she can taste and smell with her hairs and feet. Her curved, black fangs glisten as she pauses, tense and alert, inches from the mouth of her burrow. I have seen wild lions in Africa, tigers in India, and bears in America and Asia. None were more magnificent predators than she.

No fool, she realizes the Twizzle stick is a ruse. Quick as a shudder, she scoots back down into the hole. But not deep. We can still see her lurking just inside the mouth of the burrow as we leave. As we thud by her, she waits, fearless, patient, eternal as the jungle itself.

Later I asked Sam why she didn't retreat deeper.

"Why should she care?" he answered. "She's *Theraphosa*—Queen of the Jungle."

So, of course, minutes after the wasp stings, Sam swallowed some Benadryl, and we continued on. We had an appointment with the Queen.

There are plenty of tarantulas more venomous than *Theraphosa*. There are lots of spiders more venomous than any tarantula. In fact, not one species of tarantula has a bite that is deadly to a healthy adult human. (Though there are some whose bite can lay you up for a week.) In much of South America, most of the tarantula species would rather stun you than bite you. And this is actually a powerful deterrent to most tarantula predators, who tend to be smaller than humans and stick their faces farther down tarantula holes. Using rear legs to kick hairs off the abdomen, the spider counts on air currents to carry the hairs to the nose and eyes of its assailant. Because the hairs are covered with tiny barbs, they can be itchy and irritating, causing a wise predator to back away from the tarantula burrow without exploring any further.

Even the crabbiest and most venomous tarantula won't kill you. Yet the spider inspires a deep, primal awe, like we would accord a tiger or a lion.

This creature has aeons more experience at hunting and killing prey than lions or tigers do. Here is the predator primeval: Tarantulas are among the most ancient of spiders. They have lived on Earth for about 150 million years. Long before the existence of saber-toothed tigers, cave lions, and jaguars, tarantulas were the top predators—not only of their fellow invertebrates but of the early mammals too. Though surely the little Jurassic mammals ate arthropods, like spiders, the early tarantulas were almost certainly hunting these mammals too. And still, in the leaf litter of the primordial rain forest of French Guiana, tarantulas reign supreme.

French Guiana is tarantula paradise. About a dozen species of tarantula are found in this patch of jungle the size of Indiana. Every day we sought and found them, and in so doing, we rode a catapult back to the beginning of time.

In Trésor Reserve each *Theraphosa* brought a new thrill—even to Sam, who has seen so many. The first one showed us only her legs before she retreated, but even that glimpse was exciting. "Come out!" Sam pleaded with her. "I want to meet you!" And then, to Nic and me, "You know what I really want? An endoscope!" Once, he said, he had worked with an Australian spider specialist who had procured this instrument for probing human intestines and had threaded it down the twisting, dirt burrows of a different spider species. "And at the end," said Sam, "you get to see the spider biting the tip of the endoscope!" Certainly not the usual view through the instrument.

Sam shined his flashlight back in the tarantula hole. "She's hunching down," he said, "thinking, 'Oh, I really wish he'd go away!' . . . Oh! Now she's kicking! She might be kicking hairs! Can you hear her hissing?"

The brave creature! My heart swelled with admiration. Blind, cornered in her hole, this spider was ready to take us on—three monsters whose combined weight was over two thousand times hers! These spiders fear nothing. Just being with them enlarges the soul.

At another tarantula hole, a spider courageously fought

off Sam's Twizzle stick. "Strike! Strike! Strike!" Sam narrated as he tried to entice the Bird Eater out. "She's reared up and not very pleased with me. I don't think she's going to come out to play." But that was okay with Sam, because at that moment we were mapping burrows, and hers was the fifth we had encountered in just two hours. One tarantula had seized his stick and run ten inches out of her burrow, then reared up and showed us her shiny, black fangs. In another, we found a detached leg at the mouth of the burrow. Tarantulas can regrow lost legs, and at times, when a leg is injured, they will pull it off and then eat it for energy—a trick many a human athlete would envy. But this leg was part of an exoskeleton that the spider had freshly molted—like all spiders, they shed their external skeletons and grow new ones. We found the freshly molted spider deeper down the hole. Even the black fangs had been lost, the tarantula sporting newly minted white ones.

I rather wished I could molt my own skin at the end of the day. Drenched in sweat, covered in dirt and bug bites, I ached with exhaustion. So did Nic and Sam. And yet we could not have been happier. "Ah! What a job!" Sam said to us. "Can you believe we get paid to do this?"

* * *

On a different day we sought other species of tarantula. We visited a place called "Les Grottes"—the Caves. We went there with Joep Moonen, a Dutch-born botanist so skilled, he once identified a brand-new species of plant growing in a Kmart parking lot (and bestowed upon it the species name Kmartii). To reach the caves, we had to pick our way through a tunnel of rock over slippery boulders. Happily I noticed there were many handholds to steady us, but alas, we were told not to use them. Here, Joep told us, was "a great place to see fer-de-lance," and it wasn't a good idea to touch a rock beneath which one of the snakes might well be hiding. "Sometimes you might see two in one day," Joep said cheerfully. Indeed, we would be lucky to see them—until they bit, causing pain so excruciating that victims often beg to have the affected limb amputated.

We saw no fer-de-lance, but we saw another spectacular creature: a bird the color of a traffic cone who looked like he was wearing a helmet made of half an orange on his head—the male cock of the rock, one of the most dramatically colored birds in the world.

But this, of course, was not what we were after.

Carrying heavy water, camera gear, and scientific supplies (including an unsheathed cooking knife Sam used for digging that would surely impale him if he fell on it), we crossed the hundred-yard-long floor of the entry cave as carefully as we would cross a minefield. Finally, through the tunnel, we saw the great cave, our destination, yawning in front of us. It looked exactly like a giant *Theraphosa* burrow.

But we were after a much smaller quarry. The loose soil on the floor of the cave was dotted with little volcanoes of dirt—the burrows of the small, cute Holothele. Though these are among the most comment tarantulas in French Guiana, "they are in a spider family no one understands," said Sam. Another species in this family does an elaborate tap dance as a courtship ritual. Few people think of spiders as being that sophisticated, but Sam has discovered that tarantulas' lives are far more complex than anyone ever suspected. Some tarantula mothers care tenderly for their babies, for example. "Talk about family values!" he said. One species of tarantula even holds hands at dinner—mother and all her spiderlings. They feed while touching one another's tarsi, often in a circle around their shared prey.

Here in the cave we had found a sort of nursery for Holothele, though this species does not show maternal care, and the mothers were long gone. I felt a rush of tenderness as one young Holothele dashed out of its burrow, hoping to escape Sam's waiting pill bottle. He collected seven of the youngsters to bring back to his lab in Ohio, in his checked luggage—which is perfectly legal. French Guiana doesn't protect its invertebrates, and while airlines back then banned penknives in our luggage, we could carry on as many tarantulas as we wanted.

One night we went out in search of one of the most beautiful and spectacular of all spiders, *Ephebopus murinus*—the skeleton tarantula, so named for the stunning yellow stripes on its hairy, purple-black legs. Sam says they make the spider look like it is wearing a Halloween skeleton suit.

Earlier in the afternoon, while it was still light, we had located their burrows: distinctive, two-inch-wide, silk-lined funnels leading deep into the red rain-forest soil. Sam marked the burrows with orange flags, and then we left. We would need the flags to find the burrows with our spotlights that night—for it is only at night when these spiders emerge from their silky burrows to hunt.

It's a fine thing to enter a rain forest at night. Here, the darkness is warm and as heavy as velvet, and we are swallowed by it. We're surrounded with the breath of the forest, the pulse of insect calls and frog song, the occasional *quok!* of a black-crowned night heron. We thread through the jungle paths, the shapes of monstrous leaves reaching like hands toward us. Occasionally a firefly floats by. Beetles zoom past our headlamps; moths crash crazily into our faces. In the trees and on the ground we can see the sapphire glow of the eyes of the family of spiders known as Ctenids, or wandering spiders. The light-gathering reflectors in their eyes evolved separately from those of the night-hunting mammals, but for the same reason. Sometimes you can see so many of them that the ground looks like a landing strip. A female wandering spider carrying her babies on her back looks like a piece of gaudy costume jewelry, the spiderlings' hundreds of eyes glowing blue, the fire of twinkling gems.

But night can be treacherous too. It's easy to get lost here even in the daytime. A single leaf can be as big as a canoe paddle and obscure an entire path. Now, in the darkness, we find ourselves blundering into the bush. We're going the wrong way. We're sweating in the heat. The mosquitoes are swarming. But finally we find the right turn—and we see the orange flags Sam had put there earlier.

We look down—and there, illuminated in the beams of our headlamps, is the skeleton tarantula: About the size of a child's hand, she sits regal and alert on her throne of silk, just outside the mouth of her burrow. The yellow stripe on each of her eight legs reminds me of the tail of a comet. She is a starburst from the heavens, a star fallen to earth. And it makes me think of Christmas and the Wise Men's star. I feel so humbled to stand in the pulsing dark before this spider with yellow legs, this creature who tastes with her feet, who sips her prey after killing and liquefying it with her venom. All the horror and sorrow I have endured in my life now seems worth it, for this timeless, alien, electrifying moment.

After a trip like this, you go home, you want to talk about spiders. But people ask you what it was like there. What did you eat? Where did you stay? How was the shopping?

The food was unremarkable. Oddly, for a tropical country, there didn't appear to be any vegetables anywhere, except in cans. The one store we visited for food smelled faintly of gangrene. I can't remember much about what I ate except for Benadryl and aspirin. In fact, this was a major food group for Nic and me.

We gobbled these drugs to quell the itching. The forest was full of ticks and chiggers. Sam's chigger bites outnumbered his freckles and made his legs redder than his hair. But the chiggers weren't as annoying as the ticks. There were at least two species we could identify: one large, one small. The small ones were the worst, because they were so numerous and so hard to see. You found them dug into your skin in odd places on your body. Nic found one on the sole of his foot. I found one in my palm and another, one morning, inside my nose. Unfortunately an overzealous baggage inspector had confiscated my tweezers on our first stopover, in Guadeloupe, forcing me to discover a new use for credit cards: If you sandwich a tick between your Visa and your phone card, it creates just the right leverage to remove the creature. It was the only use I found for my Visa the entire trip, as it was rejected at the pharmacy in town.

This pharmacy was where we did our only real shopping. Instead of postcards and T-shirts, we bought aspirin, Benadryl, and pure rubbing alcohol, because now all our mosquito, tick, and chigger bites were infected—especially Sam's. I blamed his frightening fever on infected bites gone systemic. But it could have been something else, because before the end of the trip his right ear had swelled shut. At one point I wondered whether I too had managed to acquire a tropical fever, because I ached relentlessly every night. I dismissed this as merely muscular exertion from our day-long bush bashing, the strain of carrying heavy water and equipment up and down slippery, hole-pocked rain-forest slopes all day. I didn't know it at the time, but part of the problem was that my elbow was dislocated. At the end of each day in the field, we were sweaty, dirty, sore, and covered with so many ticks that, toward the end of the journey, I didn't even try to remove them all. (When I got home I counted my bites; there were over a hundred of them, each crowned with a little cone of yellow pus.)

And where did we stay? We spent our nights at a nature center, which had rooms with beds and blue mosquito nets, bathrooms with flush toilets and cold rainwater showers. Blessedly there was no TV, no radio, no newspaper, no war, no terrorism. The room came complete with fauna. One night as I sat on my bed, to my delight, I watched a small (and probably nonvenomous) snake crawl out of my shoe. The shower hopped with toads and frogs. Little geckos sped over the walls, clinging to the plaster with their toe pads and calling out to one another in voices that sounded like a coin tapping on glass. The mosquito nets over our beds and the walls were splashed with their red, green, or blue excrement—the color varying with what the lizard had last eaten. I fell asleep each night to the calls of jungle frogs, the watery trills of the nightjars, and the sound of my talented friend and colleague Nic, in his adjacent bed beneath his own mosquito net, scratching his bites.

"This sounds like hell!" my friends would tell me, when I got back to the States.

Hell, no. On the contrary, for me, it was heaven.

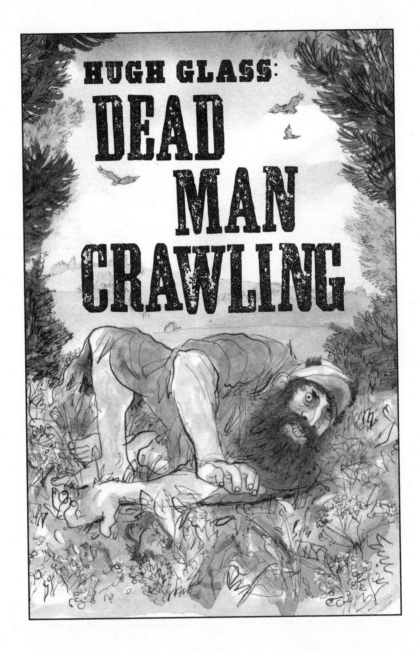

HUGH GLASS:
DEAD
MAN
CRAWLING

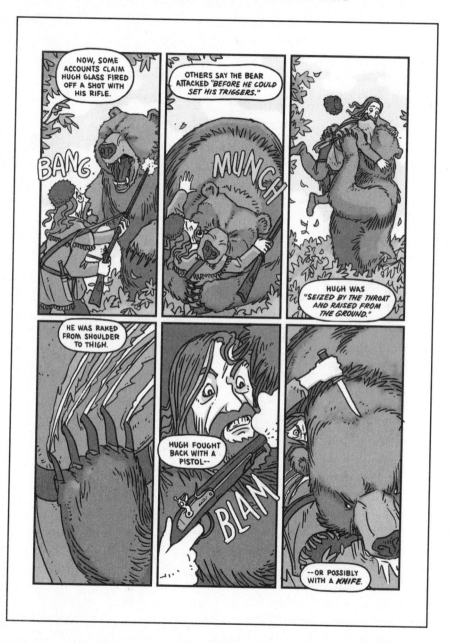

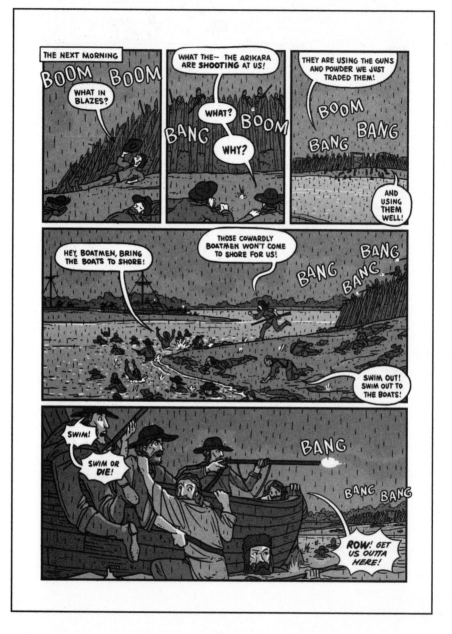

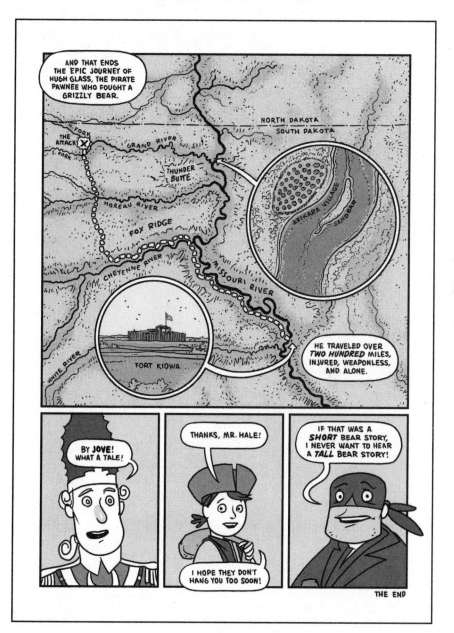

BIBLIOGRAPHY

THE SAGA OF HUGH GLASS: PIRATE, PAWNEE, AND MOUNTAIN MAN
JOHN MYERS MYERS, UNIVERSITY OF NEBRASKA PRESS, 1963

HERE LIES HUGH GLASS: A MOUNTAIN MAN, A BEAR, AND THE RISE OF THE AMERICAN NATION
JON T. COLEMAN FARRAR, STRAUS, AND GIROUX, 2012

JEDEDIAH SMITH AND THE OPENING OF THE WEST
DALE L. MORGAN McGRAW HILL, 1964

JIM BRIDGER
J. CECIL ALTER UNIVERSITY OF OKLAHOMA PRESS, 1979

COWBOYS, MOUNTAIN MEN, AND GRIZZLY BEARS
MATTHEW P. MAYO TWODOT, 2010

FOR INSPIRATION:

THE WORK OF HISTORICAL FICTION: LORD GRIZZLY
FREDERICK MANFRED BISON BOOKS, 1954

THE MOVIE: MAN IN THE WILDERNESS 1971 WHICH FEATURES A STORY INSPIRED BY HUGH GLASS'S CRAWL

HAZARDOUS TALES
ONE DEAD SPY
BIG BAD IRONCLAD!
DONNER DINNER PARTY
TRENCHES, TREATIES, MUD, AND BLOOD

NO WONDER THE STORY HAD SO MANY VERSIONS--YOU USED TOO MANY BOOKS!

YOU SHOULD HAVE STUCK TO ONE BOOK.

JIM BRIDGER APPEARS IN ANOTHER HAZARDOUS TALES STORY, DONNER DINNER PARTY, AS DOES JAMES CLYMAN. CLYMAN AND BRIDGER EACH ADVISED THE DONNER PARTY IN 1846. ONE OF THEM GAVE THEM VERY GOOD ADVICE. THE OTHER GAVE THEM VERY BAD ADVICE.

TO FIND OUT WHO GAVE WHICH ADVICE, READ DONNER DINNER PARTY BY NATHAN HALE · AMULET, 2013

JIM BRIDGER

JAMES CLYMAN

A JUMBO STORY
BY CANDACE FLEMING

On a warm, September night in 1885, the usually quiet town of St. Thomas, Ontario, Canada, teemed with people. Folks had come from miles around—by streetcar and carriage, on horseback and on foot—to see the Barnum, Bailey, and Hutchinson Circus. For days now, every fence, tree, lamppost, and barn door had been plastered with brightly colored posters promising wondrous sights: "Jo-Jo the Dog-Faced Boy . . . the Roman Hippodrome of Glorious Races . . . Nubian Warriors . . . the Bearded Lady . . . Clowns . . . Trapeze Artists . . . Mademoiselle Zarah the Tightrope Walker . . . Hagenbeck's Man-Eating Cats of Africa . . . Cinderella's Fairy Chariot . . . and more."

Despite these marvels, top billing went to the circus's

biggest star—Jumbo. "He is the biggest elephant in or out of captivity," blared the posters. "A Towering Monarch of His Mighty Race . . . Prodigious Mountain . . . Dazzling *Jumbo!*"

Those swarming to the circus that night buzzed with excitement about the elephant.

"He is all I want to see," admitted one circus goer.

"[He] is the reason I am here," confessed another.

"Oh," begged a third, "let me see Jumbo!"

Just hours earlier, circus workers had erected "a great city of tents . . . 326,000 yards of canvas" on an empty lot near the edge of town. Now, as the crowds drew near, they heard the wheezing tune of a steam calliope. Lions roared. Elephants trumpeted. The smell of sawdust mingled with the scent of animal manure and roasted peanuts.

"Step up! Step up!" called the ticket seller.

And people did. Reaching into their pockets, they dug out the fifty-cent admission. Then, tickets in hand, they wandered the midway before the performance. Many headed to the menagerie tent, where the circus animals waited for their moment in the spotlight. "Big cats and bears loung[ed] in cages," recalled one visitor, "llamas and giraffes fidget[ed] nearby." An elephant dipped its trunk into a trough of water. Was that Jumbo?

The animal keeper laughed. "Once you've seen our mighty behemoth, you will never again mistake *these* puny elephants for him," he said. "Jumbo is a gargantuan."

Leaving the menagerie, some visitors browsed the souvenir booth. Here they could choose from a vast assortment of mementos: circus programs, postcards, rubber clown noses. But the most popular items were all Jumbo-shaped: mugs, thimbles, paperweights, and coin banks. "Everyone wanted a remembrance of him," recalled the souvenir peddler.

While some shopped, others moved toward the sideshow tent. Digging another dime from their pockets, they pushed back the tent's flap and stepped into the shadowy darkness. Here, on the wooden stage, performed some of Barnum, Bailey, and Hutchinson's most famous sideshow acts: Captain George Costentenus, who was covered head to toe with tattoos—388 designs in all; Lucia Zarate, "the tiny woman," standing just twenty inches tall and weighing a mere five pounds; and English Jack, who made onlookers gasp and gag by gulping down a wiggling meal of live frogs. (Once backstage, he regurgitated the frogs that were, according to all accounts, stunned but unhurt.) It was fine entertainment. "But when shall we see Jumbo?" begged a little girl.

At last the lively strains of a brass band were heard coming from the main tent. This was the signal that the show was about to start. Following the crush, visitors found their seats beneath the big top. They leaned forward expectantly.

At exactly eight o'clock, the time when all evening performances began, there came another blast from the band.

The tent lights snapped off.

A spotlight snapped on.

The ringmaster stepped into the center ring. "Ladies and gentlemen, children of all ages, meet the most remarkable performers in the universe!"

Then . . .

"Prancing horses, tumbling clowns, bejeweled camels, elephants swaying to and fro, men and women in tights and spangles and breastplates of shining gold and steel paraded around and around in a heart-pounding display of pageantry," recalled one circus goer. "The magical beauty of it all brought tears to my eyes."

But the audience still had not seen the circus's biggest star.

Where was Jumbo?

The elephant that would become a star was born somewhere in the remote foothills of the Sudan. Snatched from his mother in 1861 by a tribe of hunters, the baby elephant was sold to a so-called "animal collector," who in turn sold him to a zoo in Paris, France. Keepers there dreamed of building an exhibit around an African elephant. While many zoos included Asian elephants as part of their exhibits, African elephants were a rarity—only two existed on the entire European continent, and none could be found in the United States. Such an unusual creature, Paris zookeepers believed, would draw huge crowds to their park.

But the baby elephant was a disappointment. Small for his age and sickly, he spent most of his time cowering in the stables. "The elephant is nothing but a malnourished runt," declared the superintendent. Frustrated, the zoo's officials gave up on their dream. In June 1865 they approached the Royal Zoological Gardens in London. Would *they* like to own a young, African elephant?

London officials leaped at the chance. They quickly agreed to trade one rhinoceros, two dingoes, a black-backed jackal, a pair of wedge-tailed eagles, a possum, and a kangaroo in exchange for the four-year-old elephant. They made this deal without seeing the animal first.

Just two weeks later, on a cloudy morning in late June, a short, muscular man sporting a bushy mustache and a tight-fitting bowler hat stepped off the train at a French railroad station.

A representative from the Paris zoo asked if he was Monsieur Scott.

The man in the bowler hat said yes, then added, "I have come for the elephant."

An assistant keeper at the London zoo, Matthew Scott had been given the job of accompanying the elephant to his new home. Chosen because of his gentleness and empathy, Scott was obsessively devoted to the animals in his care. He spent long hours, day and night, petting and talking to them. Because his animals came first, Scott had no family and few friends. "If I had not sacrificed a little comfort," he once explained, "and taken the trouble to care for them to my best and constant ability, they would not have had confidence in me. Nor would I have learned their ways. It is a fact that you cannot love, or have the affection of any . . . animal without attending diligently to its wants." This close, constant contact with the animals gave Scott an insight into their behavior that other keepers lacked. "He claimed he could talk to the animals," remarked one zoo official. "Ridiculous, of course, although he *did* have an uncanny ability to figure out what ailed a creature."

It didn't take much to see what ailed the little bull elephant the Paris representative now handed over. Bone thin and filthy, the animal limped painfully because his toenails had been allowed to grow too long. Sores covered his skin, and yellow pus oozed from the corners of his infected eyes. "I never saw a creature so woebegone," said Scott. A wave of pity swept over the keeper. Right then and there, he vowed to make things right for the elephant. "I undertook to be his doctor, his nurse, and his general servant."

Keeper and elephant took a train to the French coast, a boat across the English Channel, and another train to Waterloo station. Then together they walked through the streets of London to the zoo, the little elephant hobbling along on his sore feet. History does not record what citizens thought of the animal. But at just five feet tall and four hundred pounds, the skinny, miserable creature was hardly a majestic sight.

Scott, however, already doted on his charge. After arriving at the zoo, he tucked the animal into a "comfortable, clean bed" in the newly built "elephant stable." The scared little animal did not sleep alone. Bedded down nearby was his keeper and new best friend, Matthew Scott. "His trunk groped for my hand," recalled Scott. "Under a spell of warmth and companionship, we slept."

While the two settled in, zoo officials pondered what to name their new elephant. They eventually decided on

Jumbo, although no one knows why. *Jumbo* was not a word in the English language at that time. Most historians think it came from *mumbo jumbo,* a West African term that had been adopted by the English meaning "superstitious nonsense."

For the next several months Scott nursed Jumbo back to health, refusing to leave his side for more than a few minutes. "I watched him night and day," said Scott, "with all the care and affection of a mother . . . I took all the [infection] from his almost blinded eyes. I [healed] his scabs as cleanly as a man takes off an overcoat; and his skin was as fine as that of a horse just from the clipper's, after the hair had been cut off." He "scraped and rasped" Jumbo's rotten feet to return them to their normal shape, coddled him, and scratched behind his ears. And he led him down to the nearby River Thames to play. Sucking up the water into his trunk, the elephant would playfully shoot it at his keeper. "I got all the shower," recalled Scott, "without the ability to return the kindness. I couldn't do more than splash a bit, or throw a few buckets of water on [his] back."

As Jumbo's health returned, so did his appetite. Soon Scott was feeding him two hundred pounds of hay, three quarts of onions, two quarts of biscuits, fifteen loaves of bread, two barrels of oats, one barrel of potatoes, and dozens of apples, oranges, figs, nut cakes, and buns every day. He topped off this feast with five buckets of water and a bottle of fine Irish whiskey that Jumbo guzzled down in a single gulp. "Say what you will," remarked one zoo employee, "the elephant [has] fine taste in liquor."

Under Scott's loving care, the once puny elephant grew . . . and grew . . . and grew. By 1881 he weighed seven tons and stood twelve feet tall. And he was utterly devoted to his keeper. Following him around like a puppy, Jumbo would grow irritable and restless if he lost sight of Scott for more than a few minutes. "Jummie is a big baby," his keeper once admitted. "If I am [late] he cries and whines and becomes very naughty, just the same as a child crying after its mother." The elephant refused to obey anyone else. "Jumbo will do everything I ask him," explained Scott. "We're one—and woe to anybody who tries to come between us!"

Jumbo soon became the most popular attraction at the zoo. A gentle animal, he happily swung his trunk as he sauntered through the shaded garden or playfully squirted water at the crowds who gathered at his specially built pool to watch him drink. They tossed him his favorite treats—buns and oranges—and marveled at his size.

One person who was especially impressed was Phineas

Taylor Barnum, the flamboyant American showman. For decades Barnum had been entertaining the public with his skeleton collections and wax museums; his midgets, sword swallowers, and fake mermaids. The showman visited Jumbo whenever business took him to London. "I often looked wistfully on [him], but with no hope of ever getting possession of him . . . I did not suppose he would ever be sold."

In 1881 Barnum merged his show with those of his two competitors, James Bailey and James L. Hutchinson. Together the men created "The Greatest Show on Earth," a huge, traveling circus larger than any that had come before. Problem was, they felt they needed a fresh, astonishing exhibit to attract customers. So they sent their agents scurrying across Europe and America in search of the next great act. Months later one of those agents—Joseph Warner—returned to the circus's New York headquarters.

"Find anything over there?" James Bailey asked him.

"No," replied Warner.

Bailey persisted. "What's the biggest thing you saw over there?"

"Biggest thing I saw was an elephant in the London zoo," replied Warner.

Barnum looked up. "Jumbo?"

Warner nodded.

"How big?" asked Bailey.

Using his umbrella, Warner stretched to touch a spot high up on the office wall. "About so high."

"Are you sure?" exclaimed Bailey. He hollered to the office boy, "Eddie, get a stepladder and measure that!"

Eddie did.

The measurements stunned Bailey. "That'd make [Jumbo] the biggest elephant in the world!" he declared. "Can he be bought?"

"I'm willing to pay a fortune for Jumbo, if you could get him," added Barnum, although he doubted the zoo would sell. "That elephant is as popular as the Queen."

"Let's try to get him anyway," said Bailey. That same afternoon they telegraphed zoo officials with an offer of ten thousand dollars.

Incredibly zoo officials agreed. Despite Jumbo's generally docile behavior, men in charge worried about his temperament. African elephants had been known to become aggressive. What if Jumbo suddenly went wild? An elephant his size could cause catastrophic destruction. Better safe than sorry. "Let America have him," decided the superintendent.

In February agents from the Barnum, Bailey, and

Hutchinson Circus arrived to escort the elephant to America. Their plan was to coax Jumbo into a huge packing crate. Mounted on wheels and fortified with massive iron bands, the crate had sections that were left open so Jumbo could look out as well as swing his trunk. Once the elephant was secured inside, a team of strong horses would pull the crate to the docks, where a ship waited to sail to America.

On Saturday morning, February 18, long before visitors began arriving at the zoo, Scott led Jumbo out of his stable. The two headed toward the ramp leading up into the crate. But as they grew close, Jumbo dug his back feet into the ground and refused to move.

"Do something!" hollered one of the circus agents. He knew time was of the essence. The elephant's ship was scheduled to set sail the next afternoon. Jumbo *had* to be aboard.

Scott tried to coax his charge forward.

In response Jumbo trumpeted his unhappiness. No amount of pulling, pushing, or cajoling could budge him.

What could Scott do? "It is quite . . . impossible to move seven tons of stubborn elephant," he later said.

The frustrated circus agents sent the elephant back to his stable.

At 5:00 a.m. the next morning they tried again. Figuring

there would be few people out at that early hour, they decided to march Jumbo through the city streets to the docks.

It was still dark when Scott led Jumbo from the elephant house. Around the side of the building they trotted, the elephant good-naturedly flapping his ears. As the two came to a side gate leading to the public road, Jumbo playfully knocked off Scott's bowler hat with his trunk. The agents' hopes soared. The creature looked cooperative.

The gate creaked open, and Scott and Jumbo moved onto the road. Then Jumbo stopped. He began moaning pitifully. Speaking to the elephant in soothing tones, Scott urged him on. But Jumbo just dropped to his huge knees. He let out a cry so mournful and loud, it was heard on the other side of the zoo. Then he rolled over. Lying in the middle of the road, he grunted unhappily.

Hours passed, and a crowd gathered. "Shame!" people shouted. "Let the elephant stay."

By late afternoon circus agents gave up. All prospects of getting Jumbo to the ship on time were gone. It would be two more weeks until another sailed for America. Jumbo might as well be returned to his stable. But could Scott get the stubborn elephant to stand?

The keeper gave a sharp whistle. To the agents' surprise,

Jumbo immediately clambered to his feet. Ears flapping, he made his way through the now cheering crowd back to the elephant house.

As for the agents, they felt "utterly humiliated," recalled one.

Up until this point, zoo officials had kept the sale quiet. Had Jumbo obediently stepped into the crate, he would have been on his way to America before the public realized he was gone. But now the truth was out. And British citizens saw the elephant's refusal to leave "jolly old England" for the "uncouth wilds of Yankee America" as a patriotic act. "He is our national treasure," declared the *London Times.* "He must remain here." Seemingly overnight, citizens formed a movement to save Jumbo. Thousands of schoolchildren wrote to Barnum begging him not to take their elephant. "I do not think the children of America can be so cruel as to wish to have [Jumbo] when it makes him so unhappy to leave England," wrote one eight-year-old. Even Queen Victoria penned a letter, asking the showman to reconsider. But Barnum refused. Mourned one London newspaper, "No more quiet garden strolls . . . Our amiable [Jumbo] must dwell in a tent, take part in the routine of a circus, and instead of his by-gone friendly trots with British girls and boys . . . must amuse a Yankee mob and put up with peanuts and waffles."

Crowds descended on the zoo to say their good-byes. Many brought gifts—cakes, jams, bouquets of flowers, cookies. One elderly lady arrived with six pounds of grapes, four pounds of raisins, and a fruitcake all prettily wrapped in a ribbon-tied wicker basket. Minutes later she went away in a huff after Jumbo ignored the treats and ate the basket instead. And a nurse, knowing Jumbo faced a long ocean voyage, brought the elephant a box of seasickness pills.

Meanwhile, in the United States, excitement over the elephant grew as newspapers reported daily on all the drama surrounding him. Overnight "Jumbomania" struck. Shop windows suddenly filled with souvenirs—Jumbo hats; Jumbo earrings; Jumbo scarves, neckties, cigars, and fans. On the streets people could be heard humming the new hit tune, "The Jumbo Polka." And in restaurants diners could order Jumbo stews, soups, pies, and ice cream. "America welcomes Jumbo with open arms!" declared the *New York Times.*

If only the elephant would cooperate.

Zoo officials blamed Matthew Scott. They suspected him of controlling Jumbo with secret hand signals. "I believe his efforts to box the elephant [are] a sham," declared the superintendent. But why would Scott keep the elephant from entering the crate, or command him to lie down in the street? The reason was obvious. Scott had not been hired as Jumbo's keeper in America.

"[But] if you do this," Scott told the circus agents, "I will do my best to get Jumbo into the box."

Agents agreed.

Deal struck, Scott once again led Jumbo from the stable. This time the elephant followed docilely along. He did not dig in his heels or trumpet with fear. Instead he plodded up the ramp into the crate, where he calmly munched a peck of apples while workmen secured iron bars to the end of the box. When the crate at last rolled through the zoo gate, the elephant harrumphed. Then he held out his trunk to those who'd gathered to watch him go. Observed a newspaper reporter, "There was something peculiarly human in this attitude."

Early the next morning, Jumbo set sail for America. At his side, sitting cross-legged on the crate's hay-strewn floor, was his best friend, Matthew Scott.

Eighteen days later, on April 9, 1882, Jumbo's ship sailed into New York Harbor. Thousands waited at the dock to greet him. Cheering, they followed the still-crated elephant up Broadway toward Madison Square Garden, where the circus was currently performing.

Once there, blacksmiths set to work removing the heavy iron bands from the end of the box. Jumbo was now free. But the elephant, crated since leaving England, seemed unsure. Gingerly he lowered a foot onto the auditorium floor but quickly lifted it as if the ground was hot. Trumpeting, he backed farther into his crate.

"Be still, Jumbo," soothed Scott. "Easy, boy."

The elephant tried the other foot.

"Come on, Jummie."

Cautiously, slowly, Jumbo moved out of the box. When all four feet were on the floor, he looked around at the trapeze equipment, the Roman catapult, the three rings. Then he trumpeted again, dropped to his knees, and rolled onto his back. Joyfully he waved his legs and trunk in the air for several minutes. At last, standing again, he followed Scott to the elephant quarters at the back of the building. The circus's thirty-one other pachyderms—all smaller, Asian elephants who stood no taller than Jumbo's chin—started at the sight of the big African. "Mr. Jumbo marched along their line, saluting each one he came to," Barnum later claimed. "They seized each other's trunks, embraced, and altogether showed great delight at making a new friend."

Matthew Scott told a different tale. According to the keeper, Jumbo was completely indifferent to the other elephants as he was led to his own, separate living space. "He clearly understood that he was circus royalty," said Scott.

That same afternoon people mobbed the circus ticket office. Within minutes, all the seats for the day's performance were sold out. The audience wanted just one thing: "Jumbo! Jumbo! Jumbo!"

Barnum had not planned on exhibiting the elephant for several more weeks. He'd wanted to give both Jumbo and Scott time to settle into circus life. But with crowds clamoring and *paying* for just a glimpse of "England's pet," the showman changed his mind. For the next two weeks, while the circus remained at Madison Square Garden, Jumbo made a brief appearance at every performance. The audience was thrilled, and Barnum was seen rubbing his hands together with glee. In the first ten days, the elephant brought in an additional three hundred thousand dollars in ticket sales. (He would bring in a total of $1.5 million in his first year.) "I love that creature," gushed Barnum. He looked forward to introducing the rest of the country to his newest and greatest star.

The Barnum, Bailey, and Hutchinson Circus did not spend the entire season in New York City. There simply weren't enough paying customers for that. So after four weeks, the circus packed up and headed out on a tour of the eastern United States and Canada. Traveling by train, it crisscrossed the country in its one hundred privately owned railroad cars. Everything the circus needed was crammed in—acres of canvas and poles, costumes, cages, bleachers, thousands of posters, programs and tickets, banners and flags, instruments for the circus band, two dozen golden chariots, thousands of pounds of animal feed, and miles of electric lights as well as a power plant to illuminate them. The show's animals also rode on board—horses, zebras, camels, giraffes, ostriches, tigers, and seals, as well as the performers themselves. There were clowns, acrobats, singers, dancers, sideshow artists, daredevils, trick roller skaters, and even a tribe of cannibals claiming to be from New Zealand.

Only one performer traveled in his own personal railroad car. Red with gold edging, the Jumbo Palace Car, as it was called, was forty feet long, thirteen feet tall, and eight feet wide. It was, recalled Scott, "as big as the railroad companies permitted. Any bigger and it would not have fit through tunnels or passed under low bridges." Inside there was a separate bed and bathroom for Scott. When asked why he didn't bunk with his fellow animal keepers, Scott replied, "I need no one but Jummie."

To make the most of its time, the circus traveled at night, arriving at its next stop early the following morning. Then everyone, including the performers, worked together to haul loads and set up camp. The heaviest work was left for the animals. Horses, camels, and elephants lugged poles and dragged canvas. Only Jumbo was excused from this duty. Too valuable to be put to work, he stood watching (and eating oranges) as the circus sprang up around him.

It didn't take long for keeper and elephant to fall into a routine. Every day before the performance, Scott exercised, fed, and bathed Jumbo. He filed his toenails and rubbed lotion behind his often-dry ears. And he made sure to leave "abundant time," as he delicately phrased it, for Jumbo to "complete his business." African elephants produce up to four hundred pounds of feces a day. Just the thought of Jumbo having a bathroom accident during a performance caused circus owners to shudder. "An offering of such magnitude would clear the tent within seconds," remarked Barnum. Occasionally Jumbo's "business" did not occur by the time the show was about to start. Then Scott commanded the elephant to rear back on his hind legs a few times. This usually produced the desired results.

Performance over, Scott led Jumbo back to their train car. Before falling asleep to the rhythmic clickety-clacking of the train, the two always shared a quart of ale. It was, said Scott, "Jummie's favorite beverage." But one night the keeper forgot to give Jumbo his share. No sooner had Scott drifted off to sleep than he felt Jumbo's strong trunk curl around his waist. Seconds later he was ripped from his blankets and hoisted high into the air. "Only a promise to allow him the entire quart the following day saved my sleep," he said.

Bedding down with Jumbo could also be dangerous. One night, as the circus train chugged toward its next tour stop, there suddenly came an ear-splitting blast of whistles. Brakes squealed and cars lurched as the locomotive barely missed colliding with another train. In his palace car Jumbo bellowed with fear. Panicked, he leaned toward Scott, accidentally pinning the keeper against the wall. For one second the elephant's full weight pressed against him. The keeper gasped for air, his bones "on the brink of shattering." Jumbo seemed to recognize the danger. Stumbling backward, he pushed Scott away with his trunk. The keeper tried to laugh the incident off. "Jummie gave me such a squeeze that I don't want any more like it," he told the doctor who examined him. But the damage was done. Badly bruised, with two broken ribs and a sprained wrist, Scott spent the next six days in the infirmary. For the first time in sixteen years, Jumbo found himself without Scott at his side. Unable to perform, moping about the circus grounds, the great elephant "looked like a little girl left without its mama," recalled one circus performer.

Scott had another close call later that season. He was standing with Jumbo waiting for the performance to start when he heard a noise "like a bursting thunderstorm," he recalled. Peeking around the curtain, he was horrified to see dozens of elephants stampeding toward him, smashing everything in their path. "If death ever stared me in the face," said Scott, "it did at that moment. On came the black mass of animals, and I thought there was no escape from being crushed beneath their heavy feet."

That's when Scott felt Jumbo's trunk wrap around his waist. The elephant pulled him back behind the curtain and placed him between his massive front legs. Once the keeper was safely protected, Jumbo "stood firmly," recalled Scott, "and stretched out his trunk, as rigid as the limb of a large tree, and permitted not one elephant to get past it."

With Jumbo acting as a barricade, the stampeding elephants came to a stop. Circus workers quickly rounded them up and returned them to their enclosures. And Jumbo gently pulled Scott out from behind his legs. "He repaid me for all [the care] I'd given him by saving my life," the keeper later reflected.

For that season, as well as the next three, Jumbo was the circus's greatest star. Every night the big top (the biggest in the world, capable of holding twenty thousand people) was packed to overflowing, and hundreds of would-be circus goers had to be turned away. "Oh, please let me just see Jumbo," begged one disappointed girl. "I won't look at anything else!" When Barnum mentioned to a reporter that Jumbo liked onions, wagonloads arrived from all over the country. Fans sent loads of other gifts too: boxes of chocolates and baskets of fruit, hand-stitched quilts and crocheted pillows, jars of pickles and homemade preserves, expensive Cuban cigars, even a sewing machine. One Michigan mother named her ten-and-a-half-pound newborn baby Jumbo. The famous writer Mark Twain included Jumbo in one of his short stories. And every day mail sacks bulging with postcards and letters arrived at the circus post office. They were addressed simply to "Mr. Jumbo."

On April 30, 1885, Jumbo left New York City for what was to be the last time. As he plodded through the streets toward the train station, a crowd of thousands gathered. They whooped and waved their hats in the air. A few tossed flowers. Others threw loaves of bread. "Until next year, Jumbo!" called some. "See you next season," hollered others.

The 1885 tour season was a long one—eighty different towns in four months. The circus stopped in Philadelphia and Washington, before heading west toward Cincinnati and St. Louis. As summer faded, it moved north toward Chicago and Detroit and across the Canadian border. Both Scott and Jumbo felt exhausted when the circus finally pulled into one of its last stops—the quiet town of St. Thomas, Ontario, Canada.

Jumbo waited behind the curtain for his cue. So far the St. Thomas performance had gone off without a hitch. The trapeze artists, contortionists, and clowns in swallow-tailed coats had astounded the audience. Now, tails to trunks, the circus's thirty-one Asian elephants trotted into the center ring. Shimmering in purple and gold sequins, they rose up on their hind legs balanced on balls and formed a pyramid. Their trainer clapped his hands. Once more grabbing one another's tails, they trotted back into the wings just as a trumpet sounded.

Jumbo flapped his ears. Slowly the red velvet curtain rose toward the ceiling.

The mighty elephant at last appeared.

The audience gasped and began clapping wildly. "Jumbo! Hello, Jumbo! Over here!" they cried.

Jumbo rolled his massive head from side to side. He swung his trunk. Then with Matthew Scott leading the way, he plodded around the center ring three times. That was all. He didn't balance on a ball. He didn't wear a single sequin. "It is enough just to marvel at him," Barnum once explained.

And it was.

On their feet now, the excited audience threw bags of candy, fruits, and nuts into the center ring. "We love you, Jumbo! Hooray for Jumbo!"

Like always, Jumbo knelt and picked up one of the treats with his trunk. Brandishing it about, he acknowledged the crowd's generosity before popping it into his mouth.

The audience roared its approval.

And Jumbo, his appearance over, moved toward the wings.

Behind him a little elephant named Tom Thumb scampered into the ring. He wore a pair of striped trousers and a top hat. Known as "the clown" because of the silly routines he'd been taught, Tom Thumb comically grabbed up the rest of the goodies and dropped them into buckets. Then he hurried offstage after Jumbo.

With the crowd still cheering, Matthew Scott led both Jumbo and Tom Thumb away from the tent and along the railroad tracks toward the waiting circus cars. To the group's right stretched the Barnum, Bailey, and Hutchinson train. To their left a steep embankment sloped off into a field. Sandwiched into this narrow space, the group now walked along five hundred feet of track. Scott knew no trains were scheduled to use the track that night. Railwaymen had assured circus workers that it would be safe to walk along this stretch. Still, Scott felt uneasy. If a train did come along, there would be no easy way to escape. He tapped Jumbo's haunches with his open hand, urging the elephant to hurry.

Suddenly the keeper heard the distant rumble of a locomotive. Realizing the danger, he struggled to turn the elephants left. But they were afraid of the embankment and refused to climb down it. Frantic now, the shrill whistle of the train directly behind them, Scott slapped Jumbo's flank hard. Turning the elephants around, he began running them back toward the end of the circus train. He hoped to reach its end and pass around the front in time.

The oncoming train rounded a curve, its glaring yellow light blinding them. Panicked, Jumbo trumpeted.

The train's engineer spotted the danger on the track.

But he could do nothing to stop his locomotive. Hydraulic brakes had not been invented. All he could do was slam the train into reverse.

Wheels screeched.

Orange sparks flew.

Then . . . a sickening thud as the train plowed into the elephants. It struck Tom Thumb first. Scooping up the little pachyderm in its cowcatcher, it tossed him sideways onto the embankment. Tom Thumb screamed with pain as his front left leg shattered.

Jumbo was still running for his life when the train caught up to him just moments later. Because of his immense size, it was impossible for Jumbo to be thrown clear of the tracks. Instead train and elephant skidded together. The impact brought the train to a stop, derailing both its engine and its first boxcar. Scott, who had managed to leap to safety at the last second, was unharmed. But Jumbo lay dying.

Scrambling over the wreckage, Scott hurried to his elephant's side. Recalled one eyewitness, "The animal reached out his long trunk, wrapped it around the trainer, and drew him down to where his majestic head lay blood-stained in the cinders." Scott stroked Jumbo's face and murmured comforting words as the elephant drew one last, shuddering breath. Then Jumbo fell silent. Flinging himself onto the elephant's body, Scott sobbed uncontrollably. He lay there clutching Jumbo's motionless trunk.

Barnum heard the news hours later. "Poor Scott," he exclaimed to a newspaperman. "I don't know what he'll do without Jumbo . . . Jumbo was all the world to him." Still, the showman never let sentimentality interfere with business. He immediately sent a taxidermist named Henry Ward to the accident site. "Lose no time in saving [Jumbo's] skin and skeleton," he instructed.

Back in St. Thomas, circus workers labored to move Jumbo's body off the track. One hundred men with ropes and poles heaved and pushed for almost an hour before finally managing to tip the body of their greatest star onto the embankment. Then they set Tom Thumb's leg in a splint, packed up their equipment, and climbed aboard their train. Knowing "the show must go on," they chugged toward the next town on their tour.

As the sun rose, news of the accident spread. Crowds gathered to gape at the immense body. Local photographers took pictures. And so many souvenir hunters pulled hairs from Jumbo's tail, or chipped slivers of ivory from his tusk, that a fence was eventually built to protect the corpse. All the while Scott grieved beside his elephant. He didn't seem to notice all the commotion. For the first morning in twenty years, he didn't feed, bathe, or play with his beloved Jummie.

By that evening, news of Jumbo's death had been telegraphed around the world. In New York the *Times* headline blared, "The Great Jumbo Killed." In London the *Daily Telegraph*'s front page mourned, "Sad End of Jumbo." Obituaries appeared in newspapers all across the country. "Born in Africa in 1861, died at St. Thomas, September 15, 1885, aged 24 years," read one. "The pet of thousands and friend of all."

On the morning of September 17—less than thirty-six hours after Jumbo's death—taxidermist Henry Ward arrived in St. Thomas. He'd brought along two assistants to help with the job. But as soon as he saw the massive corpse, he knew he was understaffed. So he quickly hired six local butchers to carve up the carcass. It took them two days to remove the nearly four tons of meat from Jumbo's bones. (It was sold to a nearby meatpacking plant.) Now with just the skin, bones, and viscera remaining, Ward and his assistants began the preservation process. Standing inside the elephant's huge body, they painstakingly scraped the skin and bones clean. Buckets full of muscle tissue and other viscera were carried from the body to a nearby bonfire, where they were burned. For days St. Thomas "smelled like roasted elephant," recalled one citizen. Jumbo's heart, which weighed fifty pounds, was shipped off to Cornell University. Slices of his tusk were sent to both the British Museum in London and the Smithsonian Institution in Washington, DC. And casts were made of his teeth, showing that at the time of his death, Jumbo was still growing. Most surprising were the contents of the elephant's stomach. When Ward sliced it open, he found hundreds of coins, a handful of keys, several rivets, and a policeman's silver whistle. "Jumbo was a bank all by himself," he declared.

After three days' work, the elephant's skin and bones were ready to be moved to Ward's laboratory at the University of Rochester in New York. Here the hide was scraped to an even thickness, tanned, and stretched over a Jumbo-size wooden frame. The bones were bleached and reassembled.

When the Barnum, Bailey, and Hutchinson Circus opened for the 1886 season, it had a new and gruesome exhibit: the "double Jumbo." At every performance, the elephant's hide and skeleton were placed next to each other on a wagon. Then the wagon was pulled around the big top, followed by a long line of the circus's regular elephants. The elephants had been trained to carry gigantic, black-bordered handkerchiefs with their trunks and to stop every few minutes to dab at their eyes. It was a season-long funeral for Jumbo.

At Barnum's request, Matthew Scott accompanied the "double Jumbo." After each performance, the former keeper liked nothing better than to stand between the elephant's two frames and talk with people about his pet. "He never tired of telling of the peaceful disposition [and] kindly nature of his late chum," recalled one colleague. Many a circus goer saw tears in his eyes as he spoke.

The "double Jumbo" packed in the crowds for the next two years. "Jumbo stuffed is a greater attraction than Jumbo alive," noted a *New York Times* reporter.

But the exhibit's novelty eventually faded. Both hide and skeleton were placed in storage.

What will I do now? Matthew Scott wondered.

Barnum suggested Scott return to the London zoo. He even offered to pay for the keeper's ship passage. But Scott could not bring himself to take care of another animal. "Jummie was all," he said. Instead he remained in the United States. Renting a dingy room in Brooklyn, he eked out a living by peddling copies of his book, *Autobiography of Matthew Scott*, on the street. He drank too much and cried often. And during the cold months when the circus was at its winter quarters in Bridgeport, Connecticut, workers frequently found him skulking around the elephant house.

"Halloa, Scott," said one surprised elephant keeper, when he discovered him prowling outside the room where the stuffed Jumbo and his skeleton were stored. "What are you doing here?"

Scott begged for a moment alone with his dead friend. "[Jumbo] still talks to me," he claimed.

Noting Scott's disheveled appearance, the worker took pity and unlocked the door.

Scott slipped eagerly inside. "After a lengthy, and so far as known, silent communication with his dead friend, he at last left the place for his humble lodgings," said the worker.

But he always came back. "We see him nearly every day," said another.

Sadly Matthew Scott soon disappeared from the pages of history. By 1891 he was no longer seen selling his books or found hanging around the circus. Where did he go? Most historians believe he died around this time, although exactly where and when remains a mystery. His unusual life, however, caused one circus worker to remark, "Animal trainers, like old maids, are curious creatures."

In 1890 Barnum decided to retire the "double Jumbo." He donated the skeleton to the American Museum of

Natural History in New York City, where it is still peri-odically displayed. As for Jumbo's hide, it went to the showman's pet project, the Barnum Museum at Tufts University in Medford, Massachusetts. He had founded the museum a few years earlier, after the Universalist Church (of which he was a member) established Tufts as its first college. Becoming one of its earliest benefactors, Barnum had given the place hundreds of specimens, artifacts, and collections. Now he added Jumbo to that list.

It wasn't long before the stuffed elephant became the college's mascot (even today, Tufts' sports teams are called the Jumbos). For the next four decades, before sporting events or big exams, students made their way to Barnum Hall, where the hide stood on display. Wishing for good luck, they stuck a coin in the elephant's trunk and tugged on his tail. So briskly did they tug that in 1942, university officials clipped off the tail to preserve it. They tucked it into a box and stowed it away in the university archives.

The tailless Jumbo continued to stand in Barnum Hall for another forty years. Then, in April 1975, fire ripped through the museum. The roof and upper floor of the building went up in flames. So did Jumbo's hide.

Desperate to preserve something of their mascot, one of the museum's caretakers scooped several handfuls of the hide's ashy remains into an empty peanut butter jar. He gave the jar to the school's athletic department. To this day sports team members rub the jar for good luck. Said one athletic director, "You gotta believe that these are Jumbo's ashes. He's in there someplace. I can't tell you which molecule, but he's in there."

But the elephant's most enduring legacy is his name. Within months of his arrival in the United States, the word *jumbo* made its way into the English language. People began using the word when they meant big—*really* big. And so, in a way, the huge elephant is still with us. "Jummie," Scott once said, "will never be forgotten."

Selected Bibliography

Ardman, Harvey A. "Phineas T. Barnum's Charming Beast," *Natural History*. LXXXII, #2, February 1973, pp. 46–50, 55–57.

Bannerman, James. "The Tragic Death of the Great Jumbo," *Macleans*. November 12, 1955, pp. 28–29, 43–50, 54.

Barnum, Phineas T. *Funny Stories*. New York: George, Routledge and Sons, 1890.

_____. *Struggles and Triumphs*. Buffalo, NY: The Courier Company, 1889.

Bartlett, Abraham Dee. *Wild Animals in Captivity*. London: Chapman and Hall, 1899.

Betts, John Richards. "P. T. Barnum and the Popularization of Natural History," *Journal of the History of Ideas*. XX, #3, June–September, 1959.

Bolger, Leonard J. "Jumbo," *Natural History*. XLVI #1, June 1940, p. 8.

Chambers, Paul. *Jumbo*. Hanover, NH: Steerforth Press, 2008.

Davis, Janet M. *The Circus Age: Culture and Society Under the Big Top*. Chapel Hill, NC: University of North Carolina Press, 2002.

Edwards, W. F. L. *The Story of Jumbo*. St. Thomas, Ontario: Sutherland, 1935.

Fleming, Candace. *The Great and Only Barnum*. New York: Random House, 2009.

Goodwin, George C. "What Ever Became of Jumbo?" *Natural History* LXI, no. 1, January 1952, pp. 16–21, 45–46.

Harding, Les. "The Day Jumbo Came to Town," *Atlantic Advocate*, March 1984, pp. 45–46.

_____. "The Day Jumbo Died," in *Ontario the Pioneer Years*, ed. T. W. Paterson, Langley, British Columbia: Sunfire, 1983, pp. 26–32.

Harris, Neil. *Humbug: The Art of P. T. Barnum*. Boston: Little, Brown, 1973.

"He Saw Jumbo Killed by St. Thomas Engine," *The White Tops*, November–December 1944, p. 16.

James, Theodore. "Jumbo: Peregrinations of a Ponderous Pachyderm," *Smithsonian* 13, no. 2, May 1982, pp. 134–152.

Jolly, W. P. *Jumbo*. London: Constable, 1976.

"Jumbo-Size Bag of Bones Makes Museum Comeback,"

Roanoke Times, January 23, 1993.

Matheieson, E. *The True Story of Jumbo the Elephant.* New York: Coward-McCann, 1964.

Route Books of P. T. Barnum's Greatest Show on Earth. Unpublished. Baraboo, WI: Circus World Museum, 1882, 1883, 1884, 1885.

Saxon, A. H. *P. T. Barnum: The Legend and the Man.* New York: Columbia University, 1989.

Scott, Matthew. *Autobiography of Matthew Scott.* Bridgeport, CT: Trow, 1885.

Ward, Henry A. *The Life and Death of Jumbo: An Illustrated History of the Greatest, Gentlest, and Most Famous and Heroic Beast That Ever Lived.* Philadelphia: n.p., 1886.

UNI-VERSES
BY DOUGLAS FLORIAN

The Big Bang Theory

Some

Fourteen

Billion years

Ago, all things began,

Far as we know. The universe

Was hot and dense, and very small,

Not yet immense, but in a BANG

So BIG and GRAND all matter started
to e x p a n d and form gigantic galaxies
Of stars and planets, rocks and seas, and plants and
People, fish and frog, and me and you, and your pet dog.

The Big Bang Theory states that the entire universe was once in a very small, hot, dense state. In an explosion called the Big Bang the universe exploded and quickly expanded. After about two billion years galaxies formed, and after about seven billion years our Sun and solar system was created. The universe is still expanding and at a faster rate than before.

Physics

Physics studies
How things work,
Both quietly
Or quite berserk.
How objects move
Or groove
Or f
    a
      l
        l.
Or when they do

Nothing at all.

Physics is the science of how things behave in the universe. It studies matter and energy and how those things interact in such things as heat, light, sound, electricity, radiation, and mechanics.

Time

I wanted to write you
A poem about time,
To say something splendid
Or even sublime.
To tell time goes quickly,
But sometimes s o s l o w .
Compare time to rivers
That constantly flow.
I wanted to write that
Time can't be heard.
It cannot be seen,
Yet flies like a bird.
I wanted a poem with
Great rhythm and rhyme.
But just when I started—
I ran out of time.

Time is an ongoing progression of events taking place and can be arranged as going from the past through the present and into the future. It may also be measured in such units as seconds, minutes, hours, or days.

Relativity

The concept of relativity
Is rather simple, as you'll see.
It simply means that this and that
Are relative to where you're at.
And you and he,
And he and she,
Are relative to them and me.
And who and why,
And when and where,
Are relatively anywhere.
If you're **CONFUSED**
With what I give
Then go and ask
A *relative*.

Relativity means that the way anything except light moves through time and space is dependent on the position and motion of the observer. Also light travels at a constant speed and is independent of the observer. These theories were first proposed by Albert Einstein and have been tested since.

Matter

Matter's puzzling to explain,
But I will try, and rack my brain.
It is the substance of all things:
Protons, neutrons, electron rings.
It may have mass and volume too.
Get it?
No?

What's the *matter* with you?

Everything in the universe is made up of **matter**, from a speck of dust to the largest star. Matter comes in different states: solid, liquid, gas, and plasma. A solid has a definite size and shape. A liquid takes the shape of its container. A gas can expand to fill a container and can also be compressed. A plasma, like a gas, does not have a definite shape or volume, but it also has charged particles called ions. The Sun is mostly in a state of plasma.

Subatomic

I never wrote a poem that's comic
About things that are subatomic.
As neutrons or electron rings
Really aren't funny things.
Though there are "flavors" in a quark,
None are amusing as a stork.
For storks may make a funny sound
Or stand with one foot on the ground.
Whereas a lepton or a muon
Never tells jokes to a gluon.
(Although it's funny that Higgs boson
Romps around without his clothes on.)

Subatomic particles are smaller than atoms.
There are two types: elementary and composite.
Elementary particles are not made up of other
particles. These include quarks, leptons, and bosons,
all of which help make up atoms. A composite
particle is two or more bound elementary particles.
A proton, for instance, is made up of three quarks.
A Higgs boson is an elementary particle that carries
force within the atom.

Gravity

The opposite of levity
Supposedly is gravity.
For levity means "lightness, mirth,"
While gravity means "down to earth."
And if it simply
Wasn't there,
We'd float like blimps
Up in the air.
And though it's great,
I think, to fly,
The birds might hate
To share the sky.
And with your head
Below your feet,
It might be difficult to eat.
To see your food float out of sight
Would surely hurt your appetite.
I'll bet your sleep
Inside a cloud

Would not be deep
When things got loud.
For thunderclaps
Would hurt your head
While you were sleeping
In your bed.
Let's stick with gravity instead.

Gravity is the natural force of attraction between physical bodies. It is what gives an object weight, and causes it to fall to the ground or orbit another object with greater mass. The Earth revolves around the Sun and the Moon around the Earth because of gravity. Albert Einstein said that matter itself actually curves what he called *spacetime,* and that falling objects are moving along paths of spacetime.

Light

A definition now of light:
Something brilliant, shining, bright.
Something radiant.
Something glowing,
Helping us find where we're going.
Light's a particle.
Light's a wave.
Easy to use
But hard to save.
Light may focus.
Light may scatter.
I hope I've shed light
On this matter.

Light is the form of energy that enables us to see things. The light that we see is called the visible spectrum. This light has wavelengths from violet to red, much like a rainbow. But some animals, such as bees or reindeer, can see ultraviolet (beyond violet) light. When heat emits light it is called incandescence. Sunlight is an example. The emission of light without heat is called luminescence. A firefly uses this type of light at night to see other fireflies.

Sound

Sound is a vibration—
Waves passing right through things.
A bell of brass
Has sound waves pass
Clear through it when it rings.
Sound can move through water.
Through walls, or floors, or doors.
And through the air
At night I hear
My mother when she snores.

Sound is created when particles of matter vibrate through a material such as air, water, or a metal. The speed of sound depends on what it's passing through (the medium). Sound passes through liquids and solids faster than air, but not through a vacuum, as there are no particles to vibrate there.

Magnetism

What force may force things to attract?
It's magnetism, that's a fact.
Although two magnets may repel,
They can attract themselves as well,
Depending on the poles, of course:
There's north and south magnetic force.
When like poles face each other, say,
They push each other far away.
But when two opposite poles face,
There is attraction taking place.
A magnet picks up iron nails,
And there's magnetic monorails.
What magnetism lies in me?
Magnetic personality!

Magnetism is an invisible force of attraction or repulsion. A magnet has two poles, north and south. Opposite poles attract each other, but like poles repel. Because of its molten iron core, the Earth has a magnetic field, strongest at its magnetic poles.

Machines

Did you know that a machine
Is used to change a force?
Machines of steel can turn a wheel
Far better than a horse.

A gear, I hear,
Can help you steer
A bicycle or car.
And down an
Inclined plane it's plain
An object can roll far.

In many ways,
Throughout the day,
Machines help in the home.
And I'll come clean—
My own machine
Created this here poem.

> A **machine** is a device or tool that changes mechanical
> energy into a more useful form. A machine can change
> the magnitude or direction of a force. Many machines
> have electric motors but machines can also be
> powered mechanically, chemically, or thermally.

Velocity

Velocity is speed, you see—
How quickly fruit falls from a tree.
How fast a train may pass ahead.
H o w   s l o w l y   y o u
G e t   o u t   o f   b e d .

Velocity is the speed and direction of an object. So a car driving at 30 miles per hour in a circle has the same speed but different velocities. Acceleration is when the rate of velocity changes in regard to time.

Inertia

A body at rest will stay at rest.
A body in motion, in motion.
So you over there, get off your chair,
Or **I'll** toss you into the ocean!

Isaac Newton realized that a body at rest will tend to stay at rest, and a body in motion will tend to stay in motion. **Inertia** is the natural tendency of objects to not change their motion. So a car that is moving will continue moving unless the friction of a brake or the road touching the tires causes it to stop. Objects with more mass have more inertia. That's why it's harder to get a truck rolling (or to stop) than a bicycle.

Quantum Physics

A teensy tiny entity,
An eensy piece of energy,
Is called a *quantum*
(Plural *quanta*).
I could say more,
But just don't wanta.

Quantum physics says that energy comes in very small packets called quanta (singular quantum). Those packets behave both as particles and waves. Their movement seems random. It is impossible to know both the position and momentum of a particle at the same time. The world of atoms is very different from our everyday world.

THIS WON'T HURT A BIT:
THE PAINFULLY TRUE STORY
OF DENTAL CARE
BY JIM MURPHY

When I was six years old, my mother took me to the dentist for the first time. The dentist was a nice man with a warm, reassuring smile. He was also a family friend, so I knew and trusted him.

I remember climbing into the big chair. I wasn't nervous at all. At least I wasn't until the dentist said, "Open wide, Jimmy," and leaned in to take a look at my teeth. "This won't hurt a bit," he said as he brought a shiny, pointy, metal instrument closer and closer to my mouth.

It is hard to describe the blood-curdling sound that

exploded from my six-year-old mouth, but the scream was loud enough to make the dentist jump back. The next moment I bolted from the chair and ran out of the examination room and out of his office, trailed by the dentist, his assistant, and my mother. After circling the building twice, the adults decided I didn't have to have my teeth examined that day.

There was no good reason for my panic. No one had told me scary stories about visiting the dentist. I'd never seen a TV show or movie that depicted a mean dentist. Yet something in me—some deep-seated, primal fear—told me that a visit to the dentist could be a very painful experience.

The brief history of dental care that follows is a story of one painful and gruesome encounter after another. Before the invention of effective painkillers and advent of scientific research in the late nineteenth century, the standard treatments for bad teeth were some amazingly horrifying procedures resulting in thousands of years of excruciating pain, broken teeth, and blood. And death. Readers should be forewarned: Everything in here is absolutely true.

Now sit back, relax, and enjoy this. I promise: It won't hurt a bit.

*　*　*

Sixty-five hundred years ago, one of our Neolithic ancestors from present-day Slovenia (which is up there near northern Italy) had a toothache. It started as a little toothache, then got more and more painful as the days went along, until his mouth throbbed and pulsed and caused him excruciating agony day and night.

His family and friends did what they could to help this young shepherd. Some brewed up a hot tea of bark, leaves, and flowers. Others brought him cold, refreshing water. The problem for our twenty-six-year-old Neolithic man was that his tooth had cracked down the center and the top had rotted out, leaving the sensitive pulp exposed. Every time something hot or cold touched the pulp (in fact, every time he sucked in cool air), an agonizing electric shock of pain racked his body.

Finally someone mixed beeswax with a little honey (when honey dries out, it turns remarkably hard). Then they used a stick to pack the beeswax-honey mixture into the hole and to fill in the large crack. Almost immediately the pain began to lessen. It seemed that a simple bit of dentistry had solved his problem. Only it hadn't.

No one knew that the inside of his tooth was infected (it would be another 4,900 years before anyone discovered bacteria). Filling this young man's tooth trapped the infection inside, where it grew and caused his tooth to hurt once again. More of the delicious tea and cold water was brought to him, but it was already too late. The toxic bacteria had entered his bloodstream and quickly made its way to his heart and brain. He died a few days later, delirious and writhing in pain.

Paleoanthropologists (these are really smart men and women who study prehistoric folk) believe this beeswax filling is the first known instance of actual dental work. It may also be the first time a would-be "dentist" inadvertently killed a patient. It wouldn't be the last time.

Of course, not all prehistoric "dentists" killed their patients. Some were surprisingly skilled. Recently scientists scraped the calcified crud from between the teeth of a Neanderthal man who lived in Spain 48,000 years ago. Analysis showed someone had packed tiny bundles of plants there, which included yarrow and chamomile. Both plants helped cleanse and ease the toothache.

There's also evidence that prehistoric "dentists" in Pakistan were very good at drilling holes in teeth nine thousand years ago. They accomplished this by placing a flint-tipped arrowhead against the painful tooth and wrapping the string of a bow around it. Cupping the top of the arrow with a stone, they would pull the bow back and forth very quickly, making the arrow spin one way, then the other. It's estimated that it might take only a minute or two to drill a very neat hole through a tooth's hard enamel. By the way, when the flint tip is placed on a piece of wood, this is the same method used to start a fire. Most prehistoric tooth sufferers probably felt that a burning-hot mouth was better than a lingering toothache.

None of these nine-thousand-year-old holes had fillings in them. So why drill them? One idea is that this might be evidence of the first theory on how toothaches happened. They blamed it on worms!

A very common belief that lasted all around the world, from ancient times until well into the nineteenth century, was that very small worms were living and feeding inside the tooth. The Babylonians developed a detailed story of the worm in 5000 BC that included this delicious worm-eyed view of what it did: "Out of the tooth I will suck his blood, and from the gum I will chew the marrow."

Not to worry. The Babylonians had suggestions for a cure. They usually began by paying a priest to say prayers and provide an amulet that had been blessed. The amulet was worn around the patient's neck to drive out the worm and to insure that no new ones would drop in later for a visit.

If the pain persisted, the patient was given pulverized henbane and beeswax and told to stick it on top of the painful tooth. Warm saliva would allow this mixture to slowly dissolve, bathing the tooth with the medicine. A small amount of henbane can relax a person enough to put him or her to sleep; an overdose can put the patient into convulsions or even kill him or her. Unfortunately not many early priest-dentists knew when too much was too much.

The other cure was to take henbane or other painkiller plants, light them on fire, and blow the smoke into the patient's mouth. The notion was that the smoke would upset the worms, and they would slither to escape the tooth and mouth. Of course, some cultures took this to an extreme. The Japanese decided that if smoke was good, fire was better. They took herbal plants and combined them with cotton or wool, placed this wad on the painful tooth, and set it on fire. The hope was that the worms would die, but the patient wouldn't.

Sometimes this treatment didn't work and the pain became so horrible that the sufferer begged for relief. This usually meant removing the tooth. To accomplish this, a stick was placed against the side of the offending tooth and hit with a rock or hammer. A few solid whacks would get the job done, though shattered teeth and broken jawbones were fairly common. Cost-efficient "dentists" in Japan simply used their fingers to wiggle the tooth loose. By the way, the increase in tooth extractions might very well have resulted in a new sort of job—a dental assistant was required to hold the patient down as his or her tooth was knocked out.

Clearly enough of these treatments failed that they eventually drew the attention of authorities. Around 1772 BC a code of laws was issued by the great ruler of Babylon, Hammurabi. According to King Hammurabi, "Should a patient lose his life owing to an unsuccessful operation, the surgeon's two hands should be struck off as punishment." No record exists about Hammurabi's encounters with his day's priest-dentists, but this law suggests they probably weren't pain-free.

At around the same time, the Egyptians were establishing their own medical and dental practices. Temple priests began to train to handle all medical problems (including tooth- and gum-related ones). These physician-dentists soon came to the conclusion that worms had nothing to do with toothaches, and that prayers and blessed amulets did little good. The real problem, they insisted, was an imbalance of the body's humors. According to ancient Egyptian medical experts, the human body had four humors—yellow bile, blood, black bile, and phlegm. Without a bit of real scientific research, they decided that having too much or too little of one or more of these humors accounted for any and all medical problems, from headaches to broken bones to acne and, yes, toothaches. Like the worm-invasion idea, the theory of humors was still being accepted well into the nineteenth century.

Curing an imbalance of humors was fairly straightforward. The physician-dentist would begin by having the patient drink teas made of various kinds of bark, leaves, and flowers, including those from opium and cannabis plants. The latter two plants would certainly calm a patient but could also result in hallucinations and unconsciousness.

If the tea cure failed, they used slightly more aggressive tactics. They might have the sufferer drink a toxic mixture that could include arsenic or a poisonous plant called belladonna (commonly referred to as deadly nightshade). This would induce vomiting or diarrhea (or ideally both) to bring the humors back into balance and end the toothache.

Another technique was to use a scalpel to slice open a vein in the patient's wrist to drain off some blood. A few tablespoons of blood was thought to cure a mild toothache. More blood was drained according to the severity of the pain. No one back then had any clue about how much blood the human body contained, so physicians routinely drained so much that the patient fainted. This didn't worry clever physician-dentists; they simply declared that the patient was resting, which was another good way to balance the humors.

Naturally some Egyptian physician-dentists cooked up (literally) imaginative cures for tooth problems. One recipe found in a vast collection of medicinal cures called *The Papyrus Ebers* suggests how to create a soothing paste that would be slathered on the sore tooth and gums: "Cook the blood of a woman, and mix it into oil. Then kill a mole, cook it, and drain it into oil and follow by mixing in the dung of an ass in milk."

You might think that such a gourmet cure would drive off clients, but you would be wrong. The Egyptian diet included breads made from refined flour and cakes sweetened with honey, dates, and carobs. And when refined flour and sugar becomes lodged between the teeth, they can ferment and eat away at the enamel, causing cavities and gum disease. More and more people began to suffer from teeth and gum problems and begged for some sort— any sort—of relief.

If you had enough money, you sought out the help of

a physician. But the vast majority of Egyptians couldn't afford a professional, so they had to visit a local "dentist." And since there were no laws to regulate who could work on teeth, there were plenty of practitioners. Ordinary people hoping to build lucrative careers set up dental shops, as did butchers (who were used to cutting into animal flesh and bones) and barbers (who not only cut hair with sharp instruments, but could open a vein and drain an ounce or two of blood while a patient was on lunch break).

Other specialists and specialty items began appearing to help with a variety of dental matters. Because jewelers were used to working with tiny metal wires, they often tightened loose teeth by wiring them to more firmly anchored ones, thus creating the first braces. They also developed reusable toothpicks made out of gold, silver, or ivory to replace the old-fashioned and low-class splinter of wood or pointy quill feather. The average Egyptian could also consult an expert on their foul-smelling breath. One cure called for the patient to gargle with wine every night just before going to bed, and freshwater upon waking. For difficult cases of halitosis the "dentist" might suggest a morning rinse with the patient's own urine, though the urine of young boys seems to have been the preferred boutique item.

Ancient Greece (which lasted from 800 BC to around

150 BC) and Ancient Rome (800 BC to AD 400) carried on most of these proud dental practices—smoking out worms, purging and bleeding the humors, and gargling regularly with whatever the local "dentist" sold (see above!).

Both cultures also showed a creative streak when it came to getting teeth out of a patient's mouth. Around 400 BC Hippocrates, known as the Father of Western Medicine, described his country's advanced tooth-pulling device, which had a name that was a real mouthful—the plumbeum odontagogon. This metal instrument resembled an oversize pair of forceps. The physician-dentist would clamp the needle-nose tip around the bad tooth and wiggle it out. This was accomplished, it should be pointed out, without any sort of painkiller.

The Romans advanced the art of tooth care and extraction. Around AD 10 the young physician Celsus suggested a mouthwash of vinegar and bitter plants to ease toothache pain. When this failed (as it usually did), he suggested the area around the tooth be "cauterized with a red-hot iron."

Celsus, ever the creative chap, also came up with a new way to remove a rotten tooth. He suggested cutting the gum away from around the tooth and pulling the skin free, thus exposing the tooth's roots. The tooth could then be extracted, with either the fingers or dental forceps. Celsus estimated that the recovery time from this procedure could be anywhere from fourteen to twenty-one days.

Dental advances slowed with the weakening of the Egyptian, Greek, and Roman empires (possibly saving thousands of lives). Of course, smoking out worms, bleeding and purging to relieve tooth and gum pain, and the reliable urine gargle for fresh morning breath continued.

There were some notable advances in dentistry. The Romans filled cavities by pushing a soft, malleable metal, such as lead, into the hole. By the 1400s dentists were digging out the decayed matter in a tooth with sharp, pointed tools, then pounding in gold foil. Real improvement came in the late 1700s, when combinations (called amalgams) of mercury and one or two other metals were used. Unfortunately mercury is a poison and often leaked into the patient's mouth. Another drawback was that the amalgams had to be heated to around 200 degrees before the molten concoction could be poured directly into the cavity.

Drawing blood was still a favorite way to balance the humors and relieve a toothache, but some humane dentists found a less gruesome way to do this: leeches. A leech was placed on the gums and allowed to suck blood for up to a half hour. This took great skill, as Charles Edmund Kells made clear in 1917. "Sometimes a lively little fellow . . . will start going down the patient's throat," Kells warned, and "said patient may manifest a slight doubt as to one's being a real leech artist."

But the centerpiece of dentistry after AD 500 became the traveling professional tooth puller. Most large cities and medium-size villages in Europe had an established physician-dentist to extract teeth. Patients would lie on their backs, and the dentist would straddle them, pinning the sufferers' arms with their knees. Sometimes a dental assistant was hired to hold down the patients' legs.

But the real showmen of the tooth-drawing trade were the folk who traveled the back roads from town to town. They came in two varieties. Some traveled on their own by horseback and were commonly referred to as mountebanks. These traveling tooth-drawers would enter a village with a banner draped over their horse's rump advertising their skills. They usually carried a parasol that had a small alligator dangling from it. After a tooth was extracted, pieces of alligator tail would be used to pack the empty tooth socket of a patient.

Mountebanks collected their fee in advance and performed extractions from the saddle. They would use a long forceps to clamp on to the infected tooth, then have the horse pull away from the patient (who was usually being held by a friend or two). One advantage of working from the horse was that it allowed for a quick getaway if the procedure went wrong.

The larger tooth-drawing operations resembled a circus more than a well-organized dental practice. The troupe would set up a raised platform in the town square or marketplace. A band would play lively music to attract a crowd, then jugglers, tight-rope walkers, and puppeteers would entertain the assembled. When the crowd was large enough, a member of the troupe, called a zany, would talk up the skills of their tooth-drawer, who would then appear onstage wearing a long necklace of human teeth.

The tooth-drawer would announce he could perform painless extractions and ask if anyone had a tooth that needed pulling. Eventually a volunteer would step hesitantly forward, pay his few pennies, and sit on a tiny stool. The tooth-drawer would insert his forceps, wiggle it around dramatically, and a few drama-filled minutes later hold up an extracted tooth dripping blood for the crowd to see. It should be noted that the volunteer was a member of the troupe who had placed someone else's old tooth, plus pig's blood, in his mouth before going onstage.

After such a convincing and painless performance, reluctant toothache sufferers would begin to come onstage, though their extractions took a great deal more muscle power and created much more pain. Fortunately the cries and screams of these hapless victims were carefully drowned out by the blaring horns and the loud drumbeat of the band that always accompanied a public extraction.

Did these public tooth yankings ever cure the patient? Sometimes. If infection didn't set in, the gaping hole would eventually stop bleeding and heal itself. It might take a week or so, but the patient would be pain-free once again. Until, that is, another tooth began to ache.

Of course, some tooth-drawers came up with new and creatively cruel ways to help toothache sufferers. A Frenchman who is identified only as La Roche Operator traveled from village to village during the 1730s proclaiming a new and painless way to deal with dental problems. He took a tool ordinarily used to grip and pull a tooth and placed it on the top of the offending fang. But instead of yanking on the tool, Monsieur La Roche pounded the tool with a rock, which drove the tooth into the roof of the patient's mouth. Oddly enough, the patient felt no pain. At first. By the time he did, La Roche Operator was long gone.

Public tooth-pulling (and occasional pounding) was a thriving business for hundreds of years and lasted well into the nineteenth century. There weren't many alternatives, especially away from large cities, plus these men were very skilled at self-advertising. During the mid-1770s, a short, bearded fellow named Martin van Butchell rode around London on a white horse painted with purple polka dots. He would make frequent stops to proclaim his guaranteed method of pain-free extraction and ply his trade from the saddle. When his wife died, he saw an opportunity he simply couldn't resist. He had his wife embalmed and placed her in a large, glass case in the hallway of their home. Between the hours of 9:00 a.m. and 1:00 p.m. visitors could drop in to be introduced to the deceased Mrs. Van Butchell and, if desired, have a tooth pulled. On Sundays both Mr. and Mrs. Van Butchell rested after their long week of work.

During this golden era of tooth pulling, the practitioners—whether a physician-dentist, a barber or butcher, traveling tooth-drawer, or a local quack—managed to kill off enough people to make Attila the Hun look like a gentle sort of bloke. During one week in London in 1665, the *Bill of Mortality* lists 111 deaths caused by dental procedures gone wrong, a full 10 percent of everyone who checked out that week.

The amazing kill ratio prompted many negative responses. As early as AD 1215, Pope Innocent III suggested that real physicians leave dental work to the riffraff—"barbers, executioners, and pig castrators."

Around the same time, physicians throughout Europe began organizing guilds to promote their professions. One of the first rules implemented by a Paris guild told physicians that the people who claimed to be dentists were scum and little better than criminals, adding that guild members who worked on a patient's teeth or gums would be expelled.

These insults didn't go unanswered. Barber-dentists organized their own guilds in order to clean up their tarnished reputations. The Guild of Barbers in France suggested in 1210 that members remove the buckets of human blood that were commonly left in a shop's front window to advertise the barber's skill at bloodletting. Not to be denied a way to promote themselves, barbers soon began displaying poles with red-and-white stripes. The stripes represented the blood-soaked bandages resulting from tooth extractions.

Oddly enough, the guilds did promote a more careful approach to dentistry, warning against experimental techniques and recommending ones that seemed to work or were at least less painful and life threatening. By the mid-nineteenth century, schools were established to teach accepted dental care and do research on ways to make procedures more efficient and safe. New and safer amalgams were concocted that didn't need to be red-hot when poured into a cavity. Hand drills were replaced by foot-powered drills that eventually (in 1870) gave way to the first electrically driven drill. And finally, after thousands of years of excruciating pain, ether and nitrous oxide (laughing gas) came into general use by the mid-nineteenth century.

The age of modern dentistry was born, when truly pain-free teeth-and-gum surgery could be performed and the patients had a fairly good chance of surviving the procedure.

But the damage had been done to the human psyche. My theory is that thousands of years of agonizing dental procedures, buckets of gore, and thousands of ghastly, grisly experiments have imprinted us with a reflexive fear of the dentist, no matter how nice he or she might be.

When I went to the dentist for the second time, I was a little nervous. I had brushed my teeth every day, but I didn't floss to get out decaying bits of food. In addition, I loved to chew ice cubes and I drank great quantities of Pepsi-Cola (so much that a concerned deli owner once told me, "You know, this stuff is so corrosive, it can be used to clean bricks!"). Still, without screaming and running away, I opened my mouth and let the dentist look inside.

He poked around with one of those pointy instruments and made little grunting sounds that implied concern. He studied the X-rays of my teeth several times and seemed perplexed. When he went to get his partner, I was truly worried.

His partner looked into my mouth and seemed startled and confused. I had a saliva-sucking device hanging in my mouth, but I managed to ask, "Ith thar shomtin wong?" I braced for horrible news that would take me down the road to bloody, life-threatening dental surgery.

Both dentists looked puzzled at first. Then my dentist said, "There's nothing wrong. And knowing your history, I can't explain it. You have no cavities at all."

It turns out I have remarkably hard teeth (knock on wood) and have had very few dental problems. Even so, my heart rate goes up and I get the cold sweats every time a dentist leans in and says, "Open wide, Mr. Murphy. This won't hurt a bit."

Further Reading

I told a friend that I was writing this brief history of dentistry. He yawned and nearly fell asleep, even though I swore it wouldn't be boring. But that's the sort of respect dental history gets (or doesn't get). I think the history of tooth care is fascinating and horrifying at the same time. If you're interested, I've listed below some avenues of internet search and books that you can explore. It's the sort of history you can really sink your teeth into!

I was going to list some specific websites to check out but realized that general internet searches turn up many more interesting sites (including ones with visual images). Try out the phrases below and see what you find:

9000 Year Old Dentistry
6500 Year Old Dental Work
Prehistoric Stone Dental Drills
Ancient Egyptian Dental Care
Ancient Greek Dentistry
Ancient Roman Dentistry
History of Toothpicks
History of Gargling for Bad Breath
History of Braces
History of Dental Fillings

History of Tooth Repairs
Medieval Tooth Pullers
Traveling Tooth Pullers
Martin van Butchell

And here are some books worth looking at:

Bremmer, M. D. K. *The Story of Dentistry from the Dawn of Civilization to the Present.* Brooklyn, NY: Dental Items of Interest Publishing, 1954.

Carter, Joseph G., and Carter, Bill. *Folk Dentistry: A Cultural Evolution of Folk Remedies for Toothache.* Chapel Hill, NC: Self-Published.

Dobson, Jessie. *Barbers and Barber Surgeons of London.* Oxford, UK: Oxford University Press, 1979.

Geshwind, Max. "Wig-Maker, Barber, Bleeder and Tooth-Drawer," *Journal of the History of Dentistry* 44, no. 3 (November 1996).

Guerini, Vincinzo. *A History of Dentistry from the Most Ancient Times Until the End of the Eighteenth Century.* Philadelphia: Lea & Febiger, 1909.

Hoffman-Axthelm, Walter. *History of Dentistry*. Chicago: Quintessence Publishing, 1981.

Holbrook, Stewart H. *The Golden Age of Quackery*. New York: Macmillan, 1959.

Lufkin, Arthur. *A History of Dentistry*, 2nd ed. Philadelphia: Lea & Febiger, 1948.

Proskauer, Curt, and Witt, Fritz H. *Pictorial History of Dentistry*. Koln, Germany: M Du Mont Schaubert, 1995.

Ring, Malvin E. *Dentistry: An Illustrated History*. New York: Harry S. Abrams, 1985.

Rubin, J. G. *Dental Phobia and Anxiety*. Philadelphia: W. B. Saunders, 1988.

Thompson, Charles J. S. *The Quacks of Old London*. New York: Brentano's, 1928.

A PACK OF BROTHERS
BY THANHHA LAI

Growing up in Vietnam, I yearned to be a boy. Not a tomboy but an actual screaming, bleeding, tadpole-catching, forever-sweating *boy*. I mingled with six of them up close, daily. Six brothers. You read right, *six*! All older, all cooler, all floating around in an orbit of fun. Or so it seemed to me: the youngest, the last to attend school, the last to get a word in, the last to go to the open market alone, where snacks were guaranteed.

I didn't want to be just any boy, but a boy in my brothers' pack. They weren't individuals as much as a loud, roving whirl of privileges. I wanted in. They wanted me to disappear.

I did have two sisters. One was the oldest of us all, so

she didn't count; the other just two years older and paired as my pseudo twin. We wore matching outfits, had identical bowl-shaped haircuts, ate exactly the same food. But somehow she was so happy to be a girl. She had zero desire to snare lizards (those little suckers were fast) or wade into a pond to find betta fighting fish (there were leeches) or even take a monsoon bath (the raindrops would spear your face like arrows). My sis excelled at sewing doll clothes, molding tiny clay pots, washing vegetables, playing school. As in, she would play the teacher giving me brain-wrenching math equations. Enough said.

The pack wasn't mean. They just had longer legs and stronger arms and thus loathed to have a stumpy, round-faced baby sister trailing them. In my family the older was responsible for the younger. Thus my brothers had to protect me from the harsh sun, marauding mosquitoes, mud holes, mean ducks, and all other tropical dangers.

They were stuck with me because my mother worked. She would have preferred to stay home and mold me into an ideal girl, but my father was "missing in action," meaning the opposite side in the war had captured him. My father remains missing in action. I was one when my father disappeared, so I didn't know him to miss him. But all my life, I've tried to imagine the shock my mother must have felt. My parents had known each other since they were children.

With my father gone, my mother and oldest sister worked. That left my brothers to feed me lunch, help me with homework, and keep me halfway clean. Back then I failed to understand that they had crossed the gender line to care for me. Instead I fumed at the injustice of being a girl in a world where boys had all the fun.

That world was in the late 1960s and early 1970s in a green and humid country known for its beaches, mountains, fruit, and, unfortunately, war. My family lived in Saigon (now known as Ho Chi Minh City), the congested capital in the south. It was crowded like New York City, but as a kid I just stayed in my neighborhood and preoccupied myself with school, the open market, and my brothers.

In my experience, war wasn't scary. I lived inside a country at war, but I didn't worry about it. Bombs were not exploding above me, and people were not running around screaming. I kinda knew soldiers were fighting in some other parts of the country, and that someday tanks and guns might reach Saigon, but mostly I concerned myself with immediate injustices, like why couldn't a girl plow into objects and get scars? Or why couldn't she gobble down boiled jackfruit seeds to induce nuclear-level farts?

Every second my brothers had to watch me, it was one more second away from soccer time, lizard time, soccer time, fish-fighting time, cricket time, and soccer time. Theirs was a well-worn soccer ball I was not allowed to touch. Not to worry. I didn't even like soccer, much less a dirty, smelly ball. Why would anyone want to bounce it off his head? Or kick it endlessly from one goal to another? I just wanted to watch them. My joy, their burden.

Still, nobody whined "It's not fair" in Vietnam. That was stating the obvious. The world wasn't supposed to be fair, but you could tweak it in your favor. This sort of heavy maneuvering my brothers perfected. If they had to care for me and my twinlike sister, they would do so on their terms. My sister was easy. They would tell her to stay home and play with dolls, and she stayed and played with dolls. They would tell me to stay, and I went into sly mode. Or I thought I was sly. They saw me hiding and following them, every time.

My brothers couldn't get rid of me, so they made the handling of me a little more in their favor.

Naps

Vietnam roasted in the afternoons, so the whole country napped. Literally. Stores closed; traffic thinned out;

workers and younger students went home to rest. People usually got up at dawn, did their thing, and then napped, which revived them for the softer evening hours.

My brothers were supposed to nap too. But anyone looking at their sinewy, twitchy limbs would know they could not endure two hours of heat and stillness. I was five, just starting morning kindergarten. After lunch I napped. My brothers had a strict schedule as to who was responsible for my rest each weekday. Now, looking back, all six of my brothers have congealed into one unit. I have no idea who said or did any one thing, except that one of them was responsible.

Their routine involved tying me to a hammock hooked to posts in the middle of the living area, leaving plenty of swing space. Tying me insured that I would not fall out. Every young kid napped on a hammock in Vietnam and, most likely, everyone with brothers tied them in.

My nap helper of the day would sing three songs. After these three ear-piercing renditions, I was supposed to be asleep.

But . . .

"Aren't you going to nap?" I asked.

"I have to make sure you're asleep first." His eyes shifted to the courtyard, where no doubt my other antsy brothers were head-butting their beloved, smelly soccer ball.

"When I hear you snore, I'll go to sleep," I offered.

"*You* sleep."

"You first."

"One more song, then *be asleep*."

He sang, swinging me high, really high, almost touching-the-ceiling high. I clutched the rope tying me to the hammock, thus to life. Near the end of the fourth song, he was spitting out the lyrics.

Then silence, except for footsteps retreating from the courtyard. Definitely more than one set of feet. But what could I have done? Roped in, still whipped into the air from momentum, I lay with eyes squeezed to fight against a flip-floppy stomach. I fell asleep against my will.

Afternoon Snacks

The best part of taking a nap was waking up to a snack. Vietnam had as many kinds of snacks as it had people, and it seemed every snack was concocted from mung beans and coconut milk or was eaten fresh from the earth. My favorite was sugarcane. The cane peddler would have spent the morning chopping down each stalk, careful to wear long sleeves because the serrated leaves slash through skin like tiny swords. He'd have stripped each long stalk of its hard shell, exposing chewable, juicy flesh. Tasteless knots divided each stalk into increments. The knots had to be chopped off, leaving blocks that were one inch around and five inches tall. These were chopped further into one-inch cubes, only to be further split like wood into triangular pieces that would fit in a child's mouth. Portioned into little plastic bags, these pieces sat on ice, waiting for children to wake from their naps.

My brothers always selected the snack of the day and paid for it with the endless coins my mother left in a clear vase. Each afternoon I would beg for iced sugarcane cubes.

If I truly had been annoying, like not sleeping after three songs, they inevitably chose jackfruit for its majestic seeds and as a reminder of my outsider status. I was allowed only the yellow flesh, sweet and floral but meaningless. If I had been medium annoying, like begging for my mother's blouse to hug, the choice might have been pouches of sweet beans and fresh-squeezed coconut milk. It tasted okay. Once in a while, because my mother specifically left instructions to buy sugarcane cubes, my brothers would call to our door the old man with a pushcart that leaked ice water and transported bags of miracle.

Ah, to press that cold, cold bag to my sweaty nape. That alone would have been a treat. But get this, I got to eat the cubes. Not actually eat but chew the pulp and suck out its sweetness. When done right, I spat out nothing but chomped fiber.

In our family the youngest got to choose her share first. I picked up each bag, counting the triangles and weighing their sugary potential. My brothers banged on the table. My sister simply waited her turn.

Finally I chose. Ah, to pop the first freezing triangle into my mouth.

We were six boys and three girls, thus nine bags. My oldest sister, usually home for a nap, said snacking was beneath her. So the first to finish his or her share snatched the extra. My twinsy sister called the game unbecoming. Not me. I chewed as fast as I could, but my mouth was the smallest in the house. Inevitably one of my brothers would win by cheating. The trick called for half-chewing pieces in the first bag, grabbing the extra bag, then going back for a thorough sucking of every sweet drop in the first and a leisure contemplation of the second.

I never won, but at least I was in the game.

Haircut

In class girls sat on one side and boys on the other. At recess boys played soccer and girls jumped rope. For art boys painted and girls embroidered. I jumped rope with the best of them and sewed floral designs on many a handkerchief. I had no interest in the boys in uniforms at school. Unlike my brothers, fun was not stamped on them.

One day one of my brothers acquired a pair of scissors. Not any old scissors but one with comblike teeth that cut zigzaggy patterns.

They tried the new toy on one another. Their crewcuts, though, provided no shock value when snipped further. They needed long hair. My oldest sister, who had a glossy waterfall down her back, proved untouchable. She pinched hard, with long nails. My pseudo twin had always been so lovely, my brothers just couldn't touch her bowl-shaped page.

That left my bowl-shaped page.

A page was a bob, except shorter and rounder and uglier. In a fair universe, such a haircut would equal ample payback for all the times I sneaked out and followed the pack. And yet the world was not fair.

Two brothers dragged me to a chair. Two more held down my claws and kicks. One clamped shut my bites. That left one to snip. My hair fell in different lengths: long, short, long, short.

"That doesn't look right," one brother said.

"Cut a little more," another helped out.

"Now that side is not right," singsonged yet a third voice.

More clips. The end result made my mother scream when she got home.

The next day in class, the girls pushed me over to the boys' side. The boys scoffed and pushed me back. I then sat way in the back behind every single classmate. The day after that, I wore a hat.

My mother, hoarse from screaming, whispered that from then on at least one of my brothers must escort me to school and back home every day. They were to take me everywhere, so potential bullies would see that I had tall, sinewy brothers. They were to buy sugarcane cubes until I requested something else, which I never did. And most of all, they were to be nice to me.

These conditions were to exist until my hair regained its bowl shape. I kept my hat on much longer than necessary.

A Family Song

Anyone watching us this one evening would have glowed with fuzzy feelings. An almost cool spring night. A satisfying dinner. We were listening to the radio before bed. Elton John came on, "I hope you don't mind, I hope you don't mind that I put down in words how wonderful life is while you're in the world." One brother joined in. They all had chosen to learn English instead of French at school. Another brother joined in, voice as high as Sir Elton's.

Somehow someone flipped "I hope you don't mind" into *Hà đồ thì to má*. The lines really did sound alike. Hà is my name at home. Translation: Hà is chubby, thus has fat cheeks. Over and over the refrain went. Elton John would not stop. Neither would my brothers. Howling and singing, pausing just long enough to let me in on a secret: They had sent my school picture to Elton John and inspired this song. Now the world knew the size of my face.

My mother watched me, waiting for tears. My brothers gained momentum even after Elton John was long gone. I started to cry but instantly recognized an opportunity. I inhaled and stopped my tears. Pretending their lyrics were hilarious, I sang louder than all of them. What were hurtful words when I could be one with my brothers?

Reading

No matter how busy my mother was, she always came home in the evenings. After a dinner filled with quick-math calculations and radio time filled with deafening interpretations, my mother was ready for quiet. So we read. My brothers were responsible for selecting books from the library.

For themselves they brought home every book about every animal. For me and my twinsy sis, books about fairies and girls who won praise by doing chores. I was in first grade, reading but not fast. Vietnamese required sounding out not just every letter in a word but also every little diacritical mark around the vowels within that word. The good thing was every word looked exactly the way it should sound, so once you learned the phonetic scheme, reading was as easy as breathing.

Usually my mother got her wish. Quietly we would brush teeth, read in bed, and glide into sleep. This one time my brothers brought home *Tintin*, a comic about a boy with hair in the shape of a fishhook. A little white dog was forever by his side. I picked it up on my way to bed, intending to browse the drawings then comment on how my brothers were still stuck in picture books. But . . . the boy was clinging to a branch over a cliff, his dog climbing toward him with a rope in its mouth. The boy was on a raft surrounded by sharks, his dog barking at the fins. *Wow!!!* I ran to the bed shared with my sister and hid under the sheer sheet. I read as fast as I could, but every word took forever.

My brothers pounced. Sheet, pillows, my sister went

flying. I curled into a ball and held on to *Tintin*. My mother, whose sighs rang out between my brothers' yells, rubbed my back. I would not unfurl, so she leaned down and we whispered.

"I must read it or I might die."

"Let's leave death be, my child. The book is your brothers' choice, correct?"

"I have to. I have to. I have to."

She sat up. More sighs. "Could you allow your youngest sister this book, only for this night?"

A pounding force of explanations that undoubtedly conveyed *"Noooooo!"*

They said: The book was a one-night loan. Too many boys wanted it. It was the latest one translated from French. If they didn't return it tomorrow, they would lose their rank to be among the first ten to read the next translated issue. I had my own book. Get my sweat off theirs. They had to read it now and get to sleep. Did our mother not want them well-rested for school?

"Perhaps you can read it to her," our mother attempted.

"Nooooo!"

I too joined the chorus. I was not a baby; I can read to myself, slowly, but I can do it.

Sighing extra loudly now, our mother stated a

173

compromise. For just that night, my brothers and I would take turns reading one frame at a time. The reader was allowed the parts of the narrator and the speaking bubbles. Tomorrow my brothers would check out a back issue of *Tintin* for me and whatever else for themselves. We would all deal with future translations later.

"Either that or we all go to bed right now."

I agreed immediately. My brothers did so only after our mother threatened no soccer for a week.

We read. I couldn't really pay attention to what my brothers read because I was counting ahead to my frame and practicing each word to myself. When it was my turn to read out loud, I still stumbled while my brothers twitched and paced and groaned. What I caught of the story danced off the pages. Even my twinsy sis put down her fairy tale to listen. For once, the universe took a minuscule turn in my favor.

A Swim

Hot did not begin to describe summers in South Vietnam. The humidity dragged down your bones and enlarged your pores. A constant sticky film enveloped your skin. Add to that a dry spell where just dust and heat waves poured down from the sky, and your skin began to trap every dirty particle in the air, the way gluey tape trapped flies. The only cure was a swim. If I only knew how.

We lived near a river, making my mother very nervous. She reiterated countless times that none of us were to swim there or anywhere else. We could not even venture onto the cement bridge that spanned the river. To insure that we listened, she never bought us bathing suits.

As if that would stop a sweaty pack of boys. They learned to swim; I don't know how. While spying, I had seen them not only swim in the swirly, brown water but also dive in the shape of a croissant off the forbidden bridge. Being boys, their shorts doubled as swim trunks.

That hottest of summers I was in second grade. My baby fat was melting off, my muscles firming, and I was certain I could do anything my brothers could.

At the end of our street was our friends' house, which had the river as the backyard. Boys my brothers' ages lived there, and also a girl named Lulu, my best friend.

Not only could Lulu swim, she could hold her breath underwater longer than any of the boys, and she could climb on top of an inflated inner tube and dive deeper than them all. I cheered while standing on shore.

She knew my mom's rule, and usually she swam just a little, then climbed out and played with me. But it was an especially hot day. And she had an extra bathing suit.

In blue-and-white polka dots, I inched down the bank. The gravel stabbed my feet, but I told myself to be brave. The others had stepped on the same sharp pebbles and survived, and they were swimming and laughing, so by universal logic I should be able to too. I went in up to my knees. The water was not cool, but cool enough to instantly suck away heat. When I was up to my chest, the weight of the summer lifted. A jolt of happiness ran up my spine.

My brothers by now had noticed me. They swam closer but did not speak. I knew better than to ask for help from the pack, still mad that I had permanently invaded their *Tintin* time. It was Lulu who gave instructions. "Pedal like you're riding a bike, and claw at the water like a dog digging for a bone."

I did and sank. Somehow I could no longer find the bottom of the river. One minute I stood on mushy earth and the next I was clawing and pedaling in an expansive wet space that became wider and looser as I tried to hug it. So this was floating. It felt great. The only problem was every time I needed to take a breath, I drank the river. By the time my stomach could hold no more, I was thrashing around like a bird caught in a net.

Hands yanked me up. My body was thrown on an

inflated inner tube. Voices yelled for me to hold on. I took my first breath without water. Air, it was delicious.

I looked out at the crowd; each face was ashen, especially my brothers'. One of them said something about waiting to see if my body would float. Obviously it had not. Another said don't tell our mother. Duh! Another said quit trying to force what can't be. I got mad.

My brothers pulled my float ashore. As soon as I could touch squashy mud, I let go. They could have dragged me out of the water, but there were witnesses. They could have abandoned me, but what would they tell our mother if I went missing? They narrowed their eyes and calculated the fastest solution. I narrowed mine with equal determination. By then I was learning fairness could be maneuvered all sorts of directions.

We stared. They said something about how drowning was an awful way to go. I stood firmly on mud and folded my arms. Finally a compromise. They would teach me how to swim if I would get out within an hour. So began instructions that greatly varied from Lulu's. Not bicycle pedals but duck feet. Not doggy claws but butterfly wings. I stayed above water, mostly. The times when I did drink more of the river, I was glad to have my brothers nearby.

Learning to Bike

That sweet scene from childhood. A bike, training wheels, a helmet, a hesitant child, a soothing adult hanging on to the bike, not letting it wobble, reassuring the child that learning comes in steps and with each step the adult will let go only a little more.

I didn't get that.

It was the end of the monsoon season but not yet chokingly hot. I was in third grade and had been nagging my brothers to let me ride one of their bikes. In my memory all bikes in Vietnam came in one style—big.

This one day my brothers finally agreed, *but* no matter what happened I was to suck it up and not cry. Yes, yes, I screamed. They even told me to forgo my nap and follow them. My mouth fell open while my feet shuffled behind theirs.

That they kept pushing their oldest, rustiest bike up a long, long hill should have been a clue. But remember, I was enchanted. At the top of the hill was a bridge choked with mopeds, bicycles, pedestrians, and occasional cars, jeeps, trucks, all letting up only during nap time. A paved road ran downhill alongside houses where people lived upstairs and set up shops that faced the street: bicycle-tire repair, watch repair, French bread, fried dough, fruit shakes, and numerous offerings of sweet beans and coconut milk. These shops were closed in the afternoons.

We stopped at the highest point on the paved road, right before getting on the bridge that our mother said I could not yet cross. My brothers turned the bike around, facing it down the hill, and in unison said, "Get on."

I should have been alarmed. The paved road started high and ran on and on, but my brothers' words rang out like a spell, so I got on. The bike wobbled while they held it. I couldn't reach the pedals, but my brothers said I wouldn't need to. They had me hold on to the handlebars but neglected to mention the hand brakes. I had never sat on a bike before, so I also did not think about the brakes.

I envisioned they would hold on to the bike and run alongside me as I smiled and glided and enjoyed the wind in my hair.

I didn't get that.

Instead my brothers let go. That my hair immediately whooshed back surprised me. That I was actually sitting upright on a bike, a huge one at that, thrilled me. The paved road was long. The bike gained speed. I could feel not just my hair but my skin whooshing behind me. I was still upright. At that point my brothers yelled something about brakes. I might have replied, *"Wheeeee!"* Then I left them behind.

I finally must have lifted my gaze beyond the fast-spinning front wheel because, with the road going down down down and the bike going faster faster faster, I began to panic. How would I stop?

The bike helped out by crashing into a dessert stand. Sweet beans and coconut milk flew up and found my hair. Little bowls and spoons became birds; chairs and tables flipped over; the owners ran from the back of the house, eyes still puffy with sleep, and screamed alongside neighbors, non-napping kids, my breathless brothers, and soon the police. Let's not describe the rest of the afternoon other than to say by the time our mother returned home, the gooey beans and tapioca threads and coconut milk had congealed into a sticky hat hardening on my head. And a gigantic, blue, bloody knot was growing out of my right knee, which had hit first.

In the end our after-nap snacks ended. Those coins contributed to repairs. My brothers did not touch their, or anyone else's, soccer ball for an entire dry season. I had to spend hours bettering my vinelike penmanship.

Later, when I did learn to ride a bike, I would glide down a long hill and try to reenact that first joyride. It had happened so fast, that whoosh down the hill, my hair, skin, spirit touching the clouds. Try as I might, the feeling couldn't be recaptured. Biking was now more steady, more grounded, more predictable at every turn. At this point we had resettled in Alabama.

In April 1975, when I was ten years old, the Communists from the north rolled their tanks into Saigon and won the war. Because my father had fought for the south, my family and I had to flee Vietnam. I can't say precisely what would have happened if we had stayed, but according to my mother, my siblings and I would have become second-class citizens, not allowed into colleges, not allowed careers.

We ended up in Montgomery, Alabama, and felt as if we were second-class citizens there. In the mid-1970s it seemed we were the first Asians anyone in town had seen outside of television, which was showing continuous images of war refugees screaming and crying. The first day of school, classmates pulled my arm hairs to make sure I was real. Some shouted at me, but I didn't understand English yet. Within weeks I could guess that they were making fun of me. Probably everyone in my family was experiencing something similar in school or at work. But we didn't talk about it. We were in shock.

The kind of laughter that had made my brothers so irresistible suddenly faded; in its place lingered a tired silence.

I was no longer following my brothers around. Instead I spent hours with the Vietnamese-English dictionary in a maddening rush to cram a new language into my brain. When I did look up, I noticed my siblings were doing the same.

Within a year we were speaking English well enough to be understood. Each of us had branched out and made our own friends. My two oldest brothers went off to college, officially ending what had once been a loud, sweaty force. Even if they had remained a pack, just being in Alabama diluted my brothers' appeal. For one thing heat was missing. Alabama was actually cold during some months, forcing us into our first winter coats. Without heat we relinquished naps, wake-up snacks, year-round swims, and, without truly being conscious of it, our old selves.

Now, almost four decades later, we have all established individual lives. My brothers are scattered along the coast of California while I live north of New York City. The northeast is not known for heat waves, but once in a while in July or August this region does get slammed with a Saigon kind of heat—humid, sticky, heavy, hot. On those days I wander to Croton Landing, which overlooks the Hudson

River. No one swims in the Hudson, but sitting there, with noise and laughter coming from park goers, I can easily relive my one Saigon-river swim and my childhood days with my pack of brothers.

MOJO, MOONSHINE, AND THE BLUES
BY ELIZABETH PARTRIDGE

It was a sweltering Sunday in August 1941 when word reached Muddy Waters: A white man was looking for him. *Uh-oh*, thought Muddy. *This is it. They done found out I'm sellin' whiskey.*

Muddy was twenty-eight years old, living and share-cropping on the Stovall Plantation, deep in the Mississippi delta. Besides working the cotton and corn, trapping furs, and hopping freight trains to harvest nearby crops, Muddy made a little cash on the side selling moonshine.

It was a hardscrabble life, and what he lived for was music. Lunchtime he'd leave the fields and head to the nearest house with a radio, so he could hear Sonny Boy Williamson play live on the radio station for fifteen minutes. Muddy listened to any show with blues or church music—*King Biscuit Time, Mother's Best Flour*—he loved them all. At the local hardware store, he bought "race records"—albums made especially for African Americans—and played them on a neighbor's phonograph or at the local juke joint. If there was live music anywhere close enough to ride a horse to, Muddy was sure to show up. He learned to play the harmonica, then the guitar, sliding a bottleneck over the strings with his left hand and strumming with his right.

But today, with the white man looking for him, Muddy was worried about his moonshine, not his music. Muddy didn't want the white man finding him at home, near his bootleg whiskey stash. He headed down to the plantation store to meet him on neutral ground.

The man introduced himself, said he was Alan Lomax, and he was collecting songs all over the South for the Library of Congress. He'd heard Muddy was a good blues player, and he asked where his guitar was. Muddy was thrown off. Was this a trick by the white man to act friendly and trap him? Lomax pulled out a guitar from the back of his car, played some blues, and said he wanted to hear Muddy play. Muddy was still suspicious but agreed to go with Lomax back to his house, where his guitar was.

At the house the man asked for a drink of water and then drank from Muddy's cup. *Not a white man doing this,* Muddy thought. Whites never drank from the same cup as blacks. *This is too much, he's going too far.* In his mind Muddy was still thinking, *Oh, he'll do anything to see can he bust you.*

Lomax showed Muddy the contraption he had in the backseat: a huge recording machine. The recorder was too big to move, but Lomax pulled out the long batteries, set them on the front porch, and ran a wire to a microphone in Muddy's front room. Finally Muddy was convinced: This white man was for real. Sitting in the front room, Muddy recorded a song he'd made up earlier, "Country Blues," onto the thick glass disc spinning on the machine out in the car.

Lomax played the song back. Muddy was astonished. He thought, *Man, I can sing.* It sounded as good as what he heard on the radio. Lomax wanted to know how he'd come to make up the song. "Well, I just felt blue, and the song fell into my mind," Muddy replied. "I started to sing and went on with it." For the next few hours, Lomax recorded Muddy singing songs, some he'd made up himself, like "I Be's Troubled" and "Number One Highway Blues."

Six months later Lomax sent a check for twenty dollars

and two records, with one of Muddy's recordings on each side. Muddy carried the records up the road to the jukebox at Will McComb's café, the local juke joint. He listened to them over and over. At night, when people were listening to the jukebox, he'd sneak over and put on his music, watch them listen to it. *I can do it*, he thought. *I can do it.* He wasn't sure just *how* he was going to do it, but he was determined to quit working in the fields, get out of Mississippi, and be known all over the country for his blues.

Muddy's mother had died shortly after he was born on April 4, 1913, and he was raised by his grandmother Della Grant. When he was just a baby, crawling outside in the delta dirt, she gave him his nickname, Muddy. Della was a single woman, working as hard as she could sharecropping on the plantation. The flat, fertile delta soil had to be plowed, planted, hoed, and harvested. Anyone who was big enough to tote a cotton sack and pluck a cotton boll out of its prickly pod had to help out.

School for the black sharecroppers' kids was only for a few months in the winter, when they weren't needed in the field. By third grade Muddy was pulled out of school. Every morning he got up when they rang the 4:00 a.m. bell at the main house. He watered the cows and horses, mules and chickens, then carried buckets of water to the men and women out in the field so they could ladle out a drink. His hands blistered and finally calloused from hauling the heavy water buckets.

When Muddy was eight years old, he was handed a small cotton sack and told to start picking. Work was "sun to sun," sunrise to sunset in the broiling heat. Half the money he and his grandmother earned on the cotton went to the Stovalls, since they owned the land.

But no matter how much work there was in the fields, Sundays were church days, and his grandmother made sure he sat right next to her in the Baptist church every week. Service was exuberant, rising to a feverish pitch of singing and testifying. Muddy loved the full-throated singing and preaching. "I got all of my good moaning and trembling going on for me right out of church," Muddy said later.

His grandmother also taught him about the power of hoodoo. How Muddy could ward off bad luck and draw good luck with the right "mojo hand"—a small flannel or leather sack with roots, herbs, coins, and other "conjure" objects inside that had been "fed" by a hoodoo doctor.

Mojo, hard work, and religion mixed together as Muddy started singing spirituals and blues songs he overheard, beating time on an old metal coal-oil can. Shortly after he left school, he was given a harmonica. He carried it out to the fields, slipping it out of his pocket when he could, getting better and better at coaxing haunting, melancholy notes out of it.

But he really wanted to play the guitar. He made do by taking an old broom and unwinding the wire that held the straw in place. He tied one end to the wall and then pulled on the other end, changing the slack while he plucked at it to change the pitch.

The sharecroppers didn't have running water or electricity, but the lady across the field from Muddy had a hand-crank phonograph. Muddy was over there all the time, putting on a record, winding it up, and listening to music. He was mesmerized by blues players like Blind Lemon Jefferson, Barbecue Bob, and Son House. Muddy thought Roosevelt Stykes playing "44 Blues" on the piano was the best thing he ever heard.

When Muddy was fourteen, Son House signed on for four Saturdays in a row at a local juke joint. Muddy was there every Saturday, sitting as close as he could, watching House's hands, listening to his blues. House played a steel guitar with a sharp, percussive sound and sang in a gravelly voice. With a cut-off bottleneck on his little finger, House slid up and down the neck of the guitar. Muddy was awestruck. "That guy could just preach the blues," Muddy said. "Sit down there, and just play one thing after 'nother, like a preacher."

A few years later Muddy sold his grandmother's last horse for fifteen dollars. He gave $7.50 to his grandmother and kept the other half. For $2.50 he bought a used guitar.

Muddy practiced whenever he could, but five or six days a week he was out working in the fields for fifty cents a day. While he worked he made up songs. Like most blues, the first and second lines were the same, and the third was different. He sang about women, working the fields, the railroads, anything about the life that was going on around him. "I *always* felt like I could beat plowin' mules, choppin' cotton, and drawin' water," Muddy said. "I did all that, and I never did like none of it."

Until he could figure out how to get somewhere with his music, though, Muddy needed to figure out how to get by. After being in the field all day, Muddy went out again and set traplines for mink, possum, coon, and rabbit. The mink skins were worth good money for fur coats; the others were good eating. And when the cotton didn't need workers, there were other crops in the fields that needed harvesting: peas and beans, berries and sugar beets.

Hopping the freight trains was a good way to move

around for free, so long as Muddy kept a sharp eye out so he wasn't caught and thrown into a labor gang. While Muddy was rambling around, he came up with a song, "Rollin' Stone." "I was just like that, like a rollin' stone," he said.

Back on Stovall Plantation a tall, soft-spoken woman, Mabel Berry, caught his eye. She worked alongside him in the plantation fields and had a brother who played the guitar in a local string band, the Son Sims Four. In November 1932, when he was nineteen, he and Mabel married. Muddy had left school without ever learning to write, so he signed the marriage license with an X, and the county clerk wrote out his legal name: McKinley A. Morganfield.

By the next year Muddy was singing and playing the harmonica with the Son Sims Four. He was also learning fast on his guitar. "We played juke joints, frolics, Saturday-night suppers," said Muddy. "We was even playing white folks' parties three or four times a year." Some nights the parties went on so long, he got home just as the sun was coming up. He'd change back to his cotton-picking clothes and head for the fields.

When Muddy was twenty-two, he had a baby with another woman, and his wife packed up and left. Muddy started to host his own house parties instead of just playing at other people's. Saturday nights he'd move the beds out of the house, stick a string wick in a glass bottle, fill it with coal oil, and hang it outside. It was so quiet in the country at night, people could hear Muddy's guitar long before they got close. It was so flat out in the delta, they could see the light shining through the trees from far off. Inside there was gambling, drinking moonshine, and dancing to Muddy's music.

One night a stranger showed up at Muddy's and kept winning at dice. Muddy figured he must have a "strong mojo hand," maybe even one from Louisiana, where the hoodoo doctors made the best ones. A powerful mojo hand could give good luck in gambling, or seducing a woman, or making snakes and frogs pour out of an enemy's mouth. Muddy leaned in close to the man and slipped a pinch of red pepper in his coat pocket and secretly sprinkled salt on the floor around him. The stranger's luck turned bad, and he gambled away everything, even the shoes on his feet.

Muddy figured he'd killed the man's mojo. Instead of using his winnings for something practical, he went to a nearby hoodoo doctor to buy his own mojo hand. The doctor wrote in tiny letters on a scrap of paper and sealed it in an envelope instead of a flannel sack. He dabbed it with perfume to fix it, and told Muddy *never* to open the

193

envelope. A couple of years later, after losing all his money in a dice game, Muddy got mad and tore open the envelope. He had somebody read the paper to him. It just had "you win, I win, you win, I win" scribbled on it. Muddy had always believed in mojo, but now, for the first time, he felt like he'd been conned.

Muddy was getting so good at playing the blues that people were coming to see him every Saturday night wherever he played. He wanted a bigger audience than just the local Saturday night fish fries and local juke joints. He knew his singing and playing were good, and not just with the people around him in the Delta. Lomax had even come back a second time to record him. But Muddy wasn't sure just how to break loose.

Robert Nighthawk, a local blues player, came to see Muddy and told him he was going to Chicago. He invited Muddy to come along. "I thought, oh, man, this cat is just jivin', he ain't goin' to Chicago," Muddy said. "I thought goin' to Chicago was like goin' out of the world." He asked his friends who had been to Chicago if he could make it there with his guitar, but they told him nobody was listening to those old-fashioned blues in Chicago. It was a jazz town.

Finally, in May 1943, Muddy figured he'd better find

out for himself and bought a one-way ticket on the Illinois Central Railroad. With a suitcase in one hand and his guitar in the other, he boarded the train for Chicago.

The train slowed as it pulled into the city and chugged through miles of brick tenement buildings, the back porches built right up next to the tracks. Central Station was in the middle of the South Side, filled to the breaking point with African Americans who'd come up from the South.

Muddy had the address of his younger half sister who'd moved to Chicago. He stepped out of the train, clutching his suitcase and guitar, completely overwhelmed. "It looked like this was the fastest place in the world—cabs dropping fares, horns blowing, the peoples walking so fast." A taxicab whooshed up and Muddy got in. They sped through the streets, huge buildings looming on either side. To Muddy, the enormous apartment complexes all looked alike. How would he find his sister in all this madness?

The driver pulled up to a building, checked the names on the door, and said Muddy's sister and her husband, Dan Jones, lived on the fourth floor. There was no bell. Muddy was scared to death to be deserted in this big, frantic city, so he insisted the taxi driver wait while he walked up the wooden staircase to the fourth floor. To Muddy's huge relief, his sister and her husband were there. He retrieved his belongings from the cab and was told he could sleep on the couch.

Muddy's luck changed at lightning speed. By that night he'd found a job in a container factory. Now he had a place to stay and money in his pocket. Saturday nights Muddy's sister would hold "rent parties"—friends who'd migrated up from Mississippi would show up with a little whiskey to share and drop off a donation toward the Joneses' rent. Muddy spent the evenings playing and singing, drinking, and having a good time.

Muddy kept singing his songs about mojo, even though now he didn't believe in it so wholeheartedly. He still thought maybe if somebody got the hair off the top of your head, they could make you have headaches by burying it or putting it in running water. Maybe. But not frogs and snakes jumping out of your mouth. But he couldn't leave out mojo. It was wrapped up deep in the music, and just about everybody listening to him believed in it. There were even advertisements in the African-American newspapers like the *Chicago Defender* for hoodoo doctors and conjure materials to turn your luck around. "We played so many times, 'I'm goin' down to Louisiana/ Get me a mojo hand,'" Muddy said, "and I tried to make it a picture so you could see it, just like you're lookin' at it."

Word spread fast about Muddy. He started playing other rent parties, then house parties, where he'd be paid five dollars for the evening. Between that and his regular job, he put together enough money to get his own apartment.

Things kept breaking Muddy's way. He got his first good musical job at the Flame Club on the South Side. He'd made about seventy-five cents a day in the cotton fields; now he was earning fifty-two dollars a week playing guitar as a "sideman" for an old friend, Eddie Boyd. Eddie left and was replaced by Sunnyland Slim. Muddy quickly realized his wooden acoustic guitar was fine for the house parties, but in the crowded, noisy city clubs, he needed to be louder. He bought an amplifier and an electric guitar. By playing every chance he could, he gradually moved up from a sideman to being the leader of his own band.

Muddy even found a better day job, delivering venetian blinds. He'd get to work at eight thirty, deliver the blinds, and by one he was home taking a long nap, because he was staying up till all hours playing music five nights a week. Sunnyland Slim was offered a chance to record, and on the day he was scheduled to record, the producer decided they needed a guitar player. Sunnyland jumped on the streetcar up to Muddy's place and tracked him down on his delivery schedule. Muddy called his boss and said his mother had died and made it down to Universal Studios in time for the session. He sang two songs, "Gypsy Woman" and a song about trouble with his girlfriend, "Little Anna Mae." He didn't play bottleneck guitar but tried to make the songs fit in with a newer, jazzier style of blues. To Muddy's intense disappointment, when the songs were released they didn't sell well.

But in 1948 Muddy got another chance to record, this time with producer Leonard Chess. Muddy did a couple of his favorite delta numbers, "I Can't Be Satisfied" and "I Feel Like Going Home." This time he stuck with his bottleneck-guitar playing, singing traditional delta blues styles. The songs were released and distributed the way most race records were: copies were dropped off at a few local record stores but mostly left at barbershops, hair salons, and hardware stores.

The record cost 79 cents. The morning after its release, Muddy hustled down to the Maxwell Radio Record Company to buy a few copies. The man behind the counter would sell him only one, for $1.19, even when Muddy insisted it was his record. That day the first pressing sold out. Chess rushed to make a second pressing.

Muddy was thrilled. He'd drive around in his truck, see a bar, and go inside to check out what was on the jukebox.

Sometimes he'd get a beer and sit and listen to his song, not telling anybody it was him. Soon he started hearing it on the street, coming out of the apartments when he drove by.

Muddy and Sunnyland Slim recorded another session together, then went their separate ways. Sunnyland moved to another record label, but Muddy stuck with Chess. He thought Chess was the best man in the business. They never drew up a written contract, just had a gentleman's agreement. Chess, like Muddy, was a good judge of character. He ran his company based on good business instincts and an amazing array of superstitions. Some of his superstitions were from his early childhood in a tiny, all-Jewish village in Poland. Some he adopted from his blues players. Others seemed to have come out of thin air. Chess would never schedule a session on Fridays, or on the thirteenth of the month, but he liked the seventh or the eleventh. After Muddy's breakout hit record, Chess wanted the same bass player for the next session and insisted he wear the same red shirt he'd worn before.

Most blues players sang sad blues, but Muddy was different. He'd get out there to perform, and he'd jump on the song. It looked simple and easy, but it wasn't easy to perform with him or sing like him. He called himself a "delay singer," singing just a fraction behind the instruments. It forced his band to stay totally focused on him. They had to be ready to follow him in an instant, intuitively understanding where he was going next, before he even got there.

Six nights a week Muddy would perform wherever he was asked. He kept recording with Chess, and his records often made the national rhythm and blues (R & B) charts. In 1954 Muddy had the two biggest hits of his career, with "I Just Want to Make Love to You" and "I'm Ready" cracking R & B's top five.

There was no stopping Muddy now. He quit his job, and his songs like "Rollin' Stone," "Hoochie Coochie Man," and "Just Make Love to Me" hit high on the charts. Muddy hooked up with other blues musicians like Little Walter, Baby Face Leroy, and Jimmy Rogers. There was a side benefit as well: Women found him irresistible. Muddy married again and had babies with his wife and several with his girlfriends.

In 1953 Muddy's friend Otis Spann got out of the army and joined Muddy, playing the piano. Muddy had developed a big sound with a strong back beat on the drums, plus the guitar and harmonica and piano. "I had it in my head," Muddy said, "that the piano always was a blues instrument and belonged with my blues." All those strong sidemen gave him a full bed of music, filling up the cracks and holes, the empty spaces between his guitar and his voice. For the next ten years, Spann on the piano and James Cotton playing the harmonica formed the heart of Muddy's band.

But by the late 1950s, things started to slack off for Muddy. The blues popularity was fading fast. The African-American generation coming up, raised in Chicago, couldn't relate to hard times in the Deep South picking cotton. They weren't interested in the dark magic of hoodoo, juke joints, and bootleg liquor. It was a past they didn't want any part of. Black kids identified with the growing soul sound. Chicago blues clubs were closing, radio stations were playing soul music and rock and roll, and records by white stars like Elvis were selling like hotcakes. A friend of Muddy's, Cadillac Baby, complained, "These young people don't know nothin' about no blues, they don't feel it, they've had too good a way to go."

But Muddy still had a loyal audience in the Deep South, where he'd take his band and go on tour. "People there, they *feel* the blues and that makes me feel good," Muddy said. "They pay two, three dollars a time to come in. Mebbe they don't eat the next day, but, man, the place is really jumpin'!" No matter how he tried back in Chicago, he couldn't raise the same enthusiasm.

In 1958 Muddy was invited to tour in England. He was

eager to see what kind of audience he'd get. English teenagers were forming "skiffle bands," playing with washboard, guitar, and a simple drum set. A few had even started playing rock and roll, like the Americans. Muddy's tour was a disappointment, and he returned to an even smaller American audience.

But he was still in love with the blues and had a feeling things were going to change. A few young whites were sneaking into the Chicago blues clubs now, eager to hear him play. "I have a feeling a white is going to get it and really put over the blues," he said. "I know they feel it, but I don't know if they can deliver the message."

He didn't realize it yet, but white kids were listening to his music on records, not just in clubs in Chicago. In 1960 a young Englishman, Mick Jagger, was riding the train with a copy of *The Best of Muddy Waters* under his arm. He ran into a schoolmate, Keith Richards, whose eyes lit up when he saw the record. They went to Jagger's house and, for the next ten hours, played Muddy's music over and over again. Richards was totally inspired, as if Muddy were a codebook that opened up the whole world of blues and rock and roll for him.

Jagger and Richards decided to form a band and started practicing together. They finally got a gig, and Richards called to put an ad in a magazine. They asked Richards the name of the band, but Jagger and Richards hadn't even thought of a name yet. Muddy's album was lying on the floor by Richards's feet. The title of the first song jumped out at him, and he quickly said they were the "Rolling Stones."

To Richards, it felt like Muddy had named them. He and Jagger dove headlong into the whole American blues tradition, the darkness and trouble and hard living. "Muddy is like a very comforting arm around the shoulder," Richards said. "You need that, you know? It can be dark down there."

The Rolling Stones felt the blues, and they delivered. "We didn't think we were ever going to do anything much except turn other people on to Muddy Waters," Richards said later. "We had no intention of being anything ourselves." A lot of other young white musicians—American and English—listened to blues records, and were hungry for more. Suddenly Muddy—a real blues man—was wanted everywhere. He still played in clubs, but he was also enthusiastically welcomed at places like the Newport Folk Festival and Carnegie Hall. Before long, he was opening for rock bands in stadiums and arenas across the United States. The same blues that seemed old-fashioned to young blacks in Chicago was authentic and thrilling to white kids who'd embraced folk music and rock and roll. "I play in places now, don't have no black faces in there but our black faces," said Muddy. But he wasn't complaining.

Muddy kept touring and singing until shortly before his death on April 30, 1983. He played for all people, black and white, his powerful voice carried on simple guitar chords, a bottleneck on his little finger. His music shook awake feelings about living and dying, joy and sorrow, lust and rage. It was all there, pouring out of his guitar amp: yearning and losing, wanting and not having. It was Muddy, fueled by mojo, luck, and hard work. It was the Mississippi delta, distilled down into the deep blues.

"Man," Muddy said, "if it's warm, let's get together in the streets an' let me sing. I don't care. I'll sing my blues anywhere."

Bibliography

Muddy Waters did a number of interviews later in life. He talked about his childhood, his career, and his love of the blues. Many of the citations below include one or more of these interviews. For a full biography of Muddy's life, read *Can't Be Satisfied*.

Gordon, Robert. Can't Be Satisfied: *The Life and Times of Muddy Waters*. Boston: Little, Brown, 2002.

McKee, Margaret, and Fred Chisenhall. *Beale Black & Blue: Life and Music on Black America's Main Street*. Baton Rouge: Louisiana State University Press, 1993.

O'Neal, Jim, Van Singel, Amy. *The Voice of the Blues: Classic Interviews from* Living Blues *Magazine*. New York: Routledge, 2002.

Palmer, Robert. *Deep Blues*. New York: Penguin Books, 1982.

Rooney, Jim. *Bossmen: Bill Monroe & Muddy Waters*. New York: Da Capo Press, 1991.

Rowe, Mike. *Chicago Blues: The City & the Music*. New York: Da Capo Press, 1981.

Standish, Tony. "Muddy Waters in London," *Jazz Journal* (February 1959).

A Cartoonist's Course

BY JAMES STURM

"How do you become a cartoonist?" is a question I get regularly. It is usually asked by someone who loves comics and wants to know how to turn that love into a career. There is no short answer to this question, as every cartoonist I have ever met would respond differently. Some knew that's what they were born to do for as long as they can remember while others came to cartooning after pursuing other occupations.

My first love wasn't cartooning but dinosaurs. I owned at least a dozen dinosaur books and was transported by their illustrations. One double-page spread in particular is permanently etched into my brain: A rugged triceratops is fending off the fierce Tyrannosaurus rex as volcanoes erupt in the distance. The Tyrannosaurus rex was the aggressive bully, twice as tall as his opponent and clearly, as I saw it, the villain. The triceratops was the reluctant hero who would rather be left to peacefully nibble on primeval vegetation (but knew how to use his horned skull when provoked!).

So, in first grade, when my teacher asked the class what we each wanted to be when we grew up, I answered confidently, "A paleontologist." This was my first career choice, and I was more than pleased with myself about it. Mostly because *paleontologist* was just about the biggest word my first-grade class had ever heard, and it made me feel pretty cool explaining what it meant to all the future astronauts, baseball players, and ballerinas.

Once the thrill of feeling superior to my classmates subsided, I began to rethink my career choice. To call yourself a paleontologist, you had to do more than love dinosaur illustrations—you had to go out and find fossils. Even at seven years old, I knew that the chances of stumbling across the skeletal remains of a pterodactyl were remote. If I wanted to continue with the dinosaur thing, it had to be in another capacity. And that's when I returned to what drew me to dinosaurs in the first place: the illustrations in

that book. I figured that publishers paid someone to draw the pictures in books about dinosaurs, and that someone might as well be me.

Around this time I also picked up my first comic book. It was an issue of *The Fantastic Four*, and on the cover was a character that was orange and rocky being punched really, really hard by a much bigger guy who was clearly the villain. I wanted to know who these people were, why they were fighting, and most important who won. I must have read that comic hundreds of times. Pictures of dinosaurs fighting, while still very cool, didn't satisfy me anymore. I wanted to know the story behind the picture, and I wanted *that* story to be told in pictures too.

I quickly found out that there weren't a limited number of superheroes and villains (like there were dinosaurs) but a seemingly endless supply—and each had their own unique powers and origin. They formed groups and fought against common foes and among themselves. By the time I entered second grade, I was truly obsessed with comics and determined to become a cartoonist. It seemed like an achievable goal too, since sitting down and drawing a comic seemed a lot easier compared to searching for fossils that have been buried for a million years.

Besides *The Fantastic Four*, my favorite comics included

Avengers, Spider-Man, and *The X-Men* and I wanted the comics I made to look like them. Even then I already fancied myself a true artist—and a true artist, above all else, is original. My first order of business was to come up with my own cast of superheroes. I would spread out choice issues from my quickly growing comic book collection and open to pages that featured characters in particularly dynamic poses and copy them. But along the way I would change the costumes, turning Captain America into the Pursuer, Iron Man into the Protector, and the Black Panther into the Mighty Aeron. One character that I came up with was called Super Snotman. By shooting snot out of his nose, he could propel himself through the air. Disgusting, yes, but effective! I was sure that all these characters would soon have their own titles at Marvel.

Though drawing comics was easier than finding dinosaurs' bones, it was still a lot harder than it looked, and my early results were mixed. The superhero characters I was copying were composed of a lot of crisscrossing lines that would make the figures look three-dimensional. On good days I could make an okay drawing by carefully copying a specific pose, but the problem was I could never convincingly draw the character in any other position—I *always* needed to copy. This is a big problem if you want to make comics, because comics require that you draw the same characters over and over and over in a variety of positions.

What I wound up with weren't really comics but random drawings of posed characters. Still, I was undeterred. Cartooning was an obsession, and one good thing about an obsession is that it sort of makes you delusional. I was unconcerned that I couldn't draw cars or buildings or hidden laboratories. What did matter was that now I had at least six heroes I could draw in several positions, and that was good enough to earn my reputation as the class cartoonist. Compared to the comics I admired, my work was amateur at best, but in the opinion of my classmates, who didn't read comics, I was a special talent.

Through junior high and high school, being the only cartoonist in my class provided enough confidence for me to convince myself that I was destined for cartooning glory. But by the time I got to college, it was getting harder to sustain my delusion. In my Drawing 101 class, I struggled mightily with still lifes. In Life-Drawing Class, no matter what the size and shape of the model, he or she always came out looking like a poorly drawn superhero. Years of only copying from comic books made me ill-equipped to draw a live model. To add insult to injury, I was no longer the most talented artist in the class; in fact, I was far from it. For the first time since second grade, I began to wonder if I was truly meant to be a cartoonist.

There's nothing like the feeling of failure to open you up to greater possibilities. What else was out there besides comics? In my studio classes I tried my best to learn how to draw and not just copy. Outside the art department I took classes in history and literature, philosophy and social sciences.

As my interests expanded a friend introduced me to a stack of comics the likes of which I had never seen before. At first I didn't know what to make of them, as they were radically different from the superhero fare I had long loved. For starters, instead of being produced by a team (writer, penciller, inker), most of these comics were penned by a single cartoonist and published in black-and-white by companies I had never heard of. Some comics were drawn in a simple, pared-down style; others relished in retina-rattling details.

I later learned that these were underground comics that were published in the late 1960s. It was the first time in comics history where a critical mass of cartoonists steadfastly devoted themselves to exploring the medium's possibilities separate from any commercial concerns. Any and all subject matter was up for grabs. I read comics that espoused the virtues of feminism and Marxism and others that made fun of feminism and Marxism. I was drawn to stories that transformed the mundane aspects of life into a kind of poetry, like the wordless two-page comic of some-one doing dishes by R. Crumb. I was also fascinated by the autobiographical work of cartoonists who laid bare their own personal demons, like Justin Green, who documented his Catholic upbringing. These comics felt more intimate and honest than any I had ever seen before.

As I explored this new world I noticed that the best-drawn comics weren't always my favorites. Some comics felt so urgent that more polished artwork would have dimin-ished the story's impact. This began to make me question what actually constitutes "good" art. It made me realize that a comic is greater than the sum of its parts—the qual-ity of the drawing or writing may vary, but how the comic works all together is what counts.

No longer feeling my work had to measure up to some preexisting standard, I dove back into cartooning and began an intense period of experimentation. I drew comics where word balloons would come alive. I tried using dip pens, technical pens, and brushes. I played around with lettering and tried making comics with no words at all. I used a fine-point pen to draw incredibly tiny comics and enlarged them on a copier to see how that would affect the quality of the line.

I aspired to create complete comic books, but at the time that was still beyond my ability. I could do a few pages, but if I tried anything more than that, I would get stuck, get discouraged, and abandon the story. Four to six panels were just about all I could manage, and so I started making comic strips. I worked up the courage to submit them to my college newspaper, and when they were immediately—miraculously—accepted for publication, it was a life-changing moment.

My comic strip ran five days a week. This, more than anything else, was how I learned to cartoon. Being in print and knowing the work would be seen by others (an audience!) made me consider even more carefully how my work "read." Was it obvious which word balloon should be read first? Was the lettering big enough and clear enough? When the comic was reduced for publication, did the line work disappear? Why did people think my poodle was a rat?

Each little thing I figured out felt like a revelation. If I designed my characters more simply, it was easier to draw them in different positions; and if I lettered my comic first and *then* drew the word balloons around the words, I'd always have the required white space around the text and not have to cram letters together when I ran out of room.

Have you ever heard of the ten-thousand-hour rule? It is the idea that ten thousand hours of work is the minimum amount needed to become an expert in something. What this means to me is that practice is just as important as talent. As I cranked out my five strips a week I could certainly feel myself improving every day, week, month. Eventually I created the character that carried my strip: an egomaniacal, psychopathic pooch, Down and Out Dawg. I got a feel for pacing and dialogue. I figured out when background images were essential—and when they could be taken out.

After a few years of cutting my teeth on a daily strip, I wanted to tell longer, more nuanced stories, and I started working on two-to-three-page comics. Though a new format, my approach was the same: dive in, log the hours, and get better as you go. One new challenge that presented itself—because I didn't have a place to publish this work— was that I had no deadline. Without a pressing date by which my work needed to be ready, it was easy to get distracted. We all know there's no shortage of cable channels and video games. As I write this I've missed my deadline for this essay, and I'm sure I'd be surfing the internet or napping if this wasn't due yesterday.

So what do you do for deadlines if no one wants to

publish your work? I had noticed that many of the under-ground cartoonists who I most admired self-published. I always assumed that to become a "real cartoonist," some publishing company had to be involved. It was a radical idea to think I could publish myself—and that that might count. So when I had drawn enough pages of comics, I headed to my local copy shop and put together my own mini-comic.

It's important to note that this was during the pre-internet age; today it's even easier to publish online, since *publish* literally means "to make public." Scan your comic or take a snapshot using your phone, post it on Facebook or your school blog, and you are a published cartoonist. But back in the day, self-publishing meant a trip to the copy shop (cheap) or contracting with a commercial printer (expensive).

When I finished stapling a stack of twelve-page mini-comics, I felt like I had accomplished something of the utmost cultural importance. If even two people asked me, "When's your next comic coming out?" that was enough for me to keep going. Looking back, it seems crazy that I continued working so hard with so little encouragement. Nevertheless, I was convinced that my early, amateurish efforts would someday be recognized as lost classics.

So that's how I became a cartoonist. What I've come to realize is that my career in comics isn't the result of any innate ability or even training—not at its heart, because unless there is something driving you from the inside, you'll never get through those endless hours of practice. The reason that I am still making comics, forty years after I first declared myself a cartoonist, is because I never stopped working—because I am obsessed.

When you are obsessed with something, the answers to practical questions like "Is my work any good?" and "Couldn't I make more money doing just about anything else?" become irrelevant. These are questions asked by concerned family members and people who don't know what it's like to be engaged with something so fully that it's all you think about, all the time. When you are in the grip of an obsession, your only goal is to feed it. Quitting is not an option.

THE RIVER'S RUN
BY T. EDWARD NICKENS

"**L**ean upstream!"

My shout to my buddy Colby Lysne, sitting in the bow of the canoe, was already too late. We'd been swept into toppled trees that lined the riverbank like angry teeth, and the instant the side of the canoe dipped underwater, the roiling current flipped the boat. That's how it happened. That's how I was thrown overboard into a wild Alaskan river with ten days' worth of gear, guns, and grub. The last thing I saw before I hit the water was my pal Scott Wood sprinting toward me across an upstream gravel bar. He knew this was our biggest fear. Scott leaped into thick brush on the edge of the river, headed my way, running for my life. Then the river sucked me under, and I did not see anything else for what seemed like a very long time.

Now the world turned black and cold as the Kipchuk River covered me, my head underwater—two feet or six feet, I could not tell you—my arm clamped around a submerged tree, my body pulled horizontal in the hurtling current like a flag in a storm. Lose my grip and the river would sweep me away, into a deadly web of more downed trees and roiling current. I tightened my hold on the tree trunk as the frigid river water began to feel like a living thing, like some monster attempting to swallow me, inch by inch, and all I could do was hold my breath and hang on.

Looking back, I have to admit: I asked for it. I wanted big river adventure, and it found me.

As a kid, I didn't grow up canoeing, but once I put my hands on a paddle, my world changed. Canoes were a ticket to adventure, whether it was a two-hour expedition down a local creek or a week across the Canadian wilds. Canoes carry far more gear than backpacks—and are a heckuva lot easier on your shoulders. They open up new worlds of fishing and hunting and camping, and over the years I got pretty darn good at loading a boat with gear, guns, and fishing rods and making it down almost any river, almost anywhere. Good enough, in fact, that I started looking for rivers wild enough and remote enough that hardly anyone ever paddled them. The rivers didn't have to thunder with crazy whitewater, but the rivers I searched for needed to be off the grid, way up in the woods, out where you might not see another human being for days. For a week.

That's why I've had a few spectacular near misses and unexpected rough patches. That's why I went overboard on a stretch of river so deep in Alaska, it took tundra planes to fly in our gear—and our canoes had to be portable, packable boats that literally fit inside a duffel bag. That's how I nearly died, more than three thousand miles from home.

As the whirlpooling current sucked me under, I caught a submerged tree trunk square in the chest, a blow softened by my life jacket, and I clamped an arm around the slick trunk, tasting fear and chipped teeth.

I can't say how long I was underwater. Twenty seconds, perhaps? Forty? Later, Scott would shake his head and say: "You were being trolled underwater like a deep-diving fishing plug. I cannot believe you crawled out of that river."

For long moments I thought I wouldn't make it. I pulled myself along the sunken trunk as the current whipped me back and forth, my legs sucked straight downstream. But the trunk grew larger and larger. It slipped from the grip of my right armpit, and then I held fast to a single branch, groping for the next with my other hand. I don't remember holding my breath. I don't remember the frigid water. I just remember that the monster that was swallowing me had its grip on my shins, then I felt it clamped around my knees, and then my thighs.

For an odd few moments I heard a metallic ringing in my ears. Maybe I was hallucinating. It's hard to say. But this scary scene played across my brain: It was the telephone at home, and it was ringing, and my wife, Julie, was walking through the house looking for it. Was it on the coffee table? Did the kids have it in the playroom? It was like this weird dream, and I suddenly knew that if Julie found the phone and said hello, the voice on the other end of the line would tell her I was dead. Drowned in Alaska.

In this funky dream-hallucination I was yelling, *Don't pick up the phone! Don't pick up the phone!*

And just then, as she was reaching for the phone, the toe of my right boot dragged on something hard, and I stood up in the river, and I could breathe.

Scott crashed through the brush, wild-eyed, as I crawled to the top of the riverbank, throwing up water. I waved him downstream, then clambered to my feet and started running. Somewhere below was Colby.

The big-handed hockey player had gone overboard

farther out into the main current than I had, and had vanished beyond the strainers. Stumbling through brush, I heard Scott give a garbled cry of alarm, and my heart sank. Did he find Colby's body? I burst into sunlight by the river. Scott was facedown on a mud bar, where he'd catapulted after tripping on a root. His paddling partner, Edwin Aguilar, battered his way out of a nearby thicket. A few feet away Colby stood chest-deep in the river, with stunned eyes and mouth open, marvelously alive. In his hand he gripped the bowline to the canoe, half-sunk and turned on its side, gear bags held fast with rope.

Our ragged little foursome huddled by the river, dumbstruck by our good luck. For a long time we simply shook our heads and tried not to meet the fear in one another's eyes.

I'd lost a shotgun, two fly rods and reels, and a grab bag of gear, but everything else that went into the river had come out.

Edwin walked over quietly. He knew how close I'd come. "You okay?" he asked. "I mean, in your head?"

Just then the thing that felt cool and wet and slithery slid down my legs and off my body. I began to shiver, and no one said a word.

That was a pretty rough few minutes, I'll admit.

But here's what happened next—and this happens a lot. On so many river trips, the best fishing seems to come after the worst stretches of river.

A few miles downstream we ran into a big set of rapids, too heavy to chance running with loaded boats. Using ropes tied to each end of the canoes, we "lined" the craft through the angry water, then dragged the canoes to the head of a deep pool the color of smoke and emeralds. It was the first utterly green, seemingly bottomless pool we'd seen, and a half dozen very large salmon held motionless near the upstream ledge. While my river mates coiled ropes, I quietly slid a rod out of the canoe. The first cast landed a pink salmon. My second brought in a chum salmon. I hooted with guilty pleasure as the fish leaped into the sunlight. My pals grabbed their fly rods.

Within minutes total fishing chaos broke out on the riverbank. Scott, Colby, and I worked a triple hookup on salmon, our lines crossing. We fought sockeyes, kings, and wolf-fanged chum salmon with garish spawning teeth erupting through the gums. We landed cookie-gutter three-pound Arctic grayling and a solid twenty-six-inch rainbow trout. The fish ran up the frothy, white rapids at the head of the pool, leaping like silver and purple kites, at times so close that they splashed us with their tails.

"This is the outrageous, end-of-the-world fishing bomb!" Edwin shouted, standing on a cairn of stacked cobble as his rod curved steeply toward the pool.

For the first time I felt the pieces coming together. The pull of strong fish was medicine for ragged nerves and sore shoulders. Later that night eleven king salmon steaks slathered in chipotle sauce sizzled over the fire. Snow hung in the hollows of the high tundra hills above us.

"We deserved today," Edwin said, lying back on a bed of rocks.

And how.

On the Kipchuk River we knew we were headed for water where anything could happen. We purposefully picked a stretch of river where there were hardly any records of canoeists on the stream. But not every river has to be that crazy-wild to have its share of adrenaline-pumping moments. Sometimes you're right in the middle of an everyday paddle stroke and everything's going just fine—until the river has other ideas.

Once, my buddy Peter DeJong and I cracked a wacky scheme. Walleyes are bug-eyed, copper-colored fish best known as being from big, deep, Canadian waters. When most people think of walleye fishing, they think of big lakes, big outboard motors, and trolling baits so deep, the fish they catch need eyeballs the size of gumdrops.

But Peter and I knew that not all walleyes hung out in white-capped lakes. We figured there were river walleyes far up in the Canadian north that rarely saw a hook, never heard a motor, and shared waters with pike, moose, and sandhill cranes. Peter is a big, burly, bearded Canadian, the kind of guy who wears wool plaid shirts when it's 90 degrees outside. Together we hatched a big, burly river trip in the style of the old voyageurs, those wool-and-fringed-leather-wearing French fur trappers who paddled birchbark canoes a couple centuries ago. We'd run a few moderate whitewater rapids, cross empty lakes, hump our gear through bogs and woods, and fish our way through far northern Ontario. And we'd do it along one of the most historic fur-trading routes in all of Canada.

By now maybe you've figured out that this story is all about things that go wrong and ugly and upside down on a river, so here it comes. Our first big challenge on the Missinaibi River—other than finding fish—came during our second day. Greenhill Rapids is a three-quarter-mile-long rapid that rips and roars across an esker, a weird rock formation created thousands of years ago when a receding glacier piled up a bunch of massive rocks. There's a dog-leg turn in the middle of the rapids and canoe-swamping boulders all the way down. At low water it's almost too low to run, at high water it's crazy, and when the water is just right, you'd better be on top of your game. No surprise, then, that we played it safe, portaging our gear.

Portaging is a pretty fancy word for a pretty simple idea: We carried all our stuff around the rapids—humping every bag, pack, and rod for a mile across hill and bog. That left us with an empty boat to paddle through the rapids. As Peter and I pushed off, my tongue was as dry as toast.

We ran the big upper drops pretty clean, bashing through high rollers, then pulled in behind a midstream boulder to catch our breaths. From there on out, there were drops, rocks, and suckholes aplenty, but a kinda-sorta obvious route through the rough stuff. "A walk in the park," Peter said nervously.

That's when the wheels came off the bus. I gave the canoe a strong forward stroke to reenter the hard-charging river but screwed up my downstream lean. The canoe jerked violently to the right. As I was going over I got a glance at Peter, bracing the canoe from the bow, but he knew the goose was cooked. In half a second we were in the water, the boat between us like a giant battering ram, everything and everybody out of control.

For a couple of minutes it seemed like no big deal. We

roller-coastered up and down tall waves for three hundred yards, but then bigger boulders and nasty ledge drops showed up. The canoe suddenly lurched to a stop, pinned against a rock the size of a pickup truck. The current washed me past the canoe just as I made a desperate grab for a gunwale. Upstream, Peter slipped over a ledge and bobbed to the surface. My "okay" sign let him know I wasn't hurt, and he returned it with a humiliated grin. That's when he slammed into an underwater boulder. He hit it hard, the kind of hard that makes you think of bones poking out of skin and rescue helicopters. His grin instantly turned into an O of pain. He slid over a hump of foaming water and came to an instant stop, his body downstream, right leg pointing upriver. I couldn't believe it. With one foot trapped in the rocks on the river bottom, the Missinaibi poured over his shoulders.

Twenty yards downstream I could do nothing but watch as he struggled to right himself and keep his head above water. If his free leg slipped, the current would sweep him downstream and snap his leg like a pencil, if it wasn't broken already. Peter strained against the river current, at times completely submerged, as he tried to twist his leg out of the snare.

Suddenly he wrenched himself free. He worked across

the river carefully, grimacing, as I grabbed a rescue rope in case he stumbled again. He made it to the overturned canoe wild-eyed and panting, soaked and starting to chill. "I'm all right," he said. For a full minute neither of us spoke another word. "Strange way to catch a walleye, eh?" he said. We laughed the nervous laugh of a couple of guys who knew they had dodged a bullet.

That trip ended up pretty swell, though. We caught tons of fish and grilled them over cedar-wood fires and camped on rocky cliffs where you could hardly hear yourself think for the thundering water below. We did end up trying to take a wilderness shortcut, and it's no surprise that turned into a mess. Our shortcut required a mile-long portage through a lily-pad-choked bog. There's nothing less fun than trying to slap mosquitoes while balancing a seventy-five-pound boat on your shoulders.

Come to think of it, though, the Missinaibi River was nothing compared to the Rocky Tangle. Holy catfish, that was a rough one. Some of my hairiest times in a canoe have occurred when the canoe was actually over my head. On my shoulders, to be exact.

The Rocky Tangle was our name for a monster portage route that took me and my pals almost two full days to complete. It wasn't rapids that forced us to walk this time.

The river literally disappeared into the ground beneath our feet.

We were on the Kanairiktok River in northern Labrador. This is one of those places you might not even know exists, a chunk of far eastern Canada that might be wilder than Alaska. Just getting there took some doing. First we logged thirteen hundred miles on a jet to Sept-Îles, Quebec, on the shores of the Saint Lawrence River. There we crowded onto a train slammed full of caribou hunters and Innu natives for a twelve-hour, dawn-to-dusk train ride to an old mining camp right on the Labrador line. On day three a rusty school-bus-turned-taxi loaded down with bloody caribou antlers delivered us to a floatplane base outside the village. And from *there* we took to the skies again for a 135-mile floatplane flight to a skinny lake so far up the Kanairiktok River that it wasn't really a river yet. That's where the real travel began: from lake to pond to lake to river, by canoe and hiking boot and waders.

We'd been on the waterway for several days when the river vanished. Seriously. It just gurgled away into the ground. Over a quarter of a mile the river got wider and wider; then it flowed into a gargantuan boulder field that was topped with shrubs and patches of tundra. Hopping from rock to rock, we could see the river under our feet—sometimes fifteen feet under our feet.

To get packs and canoes around the mess, we cut cross-country, through tundra and taiga, tied to the canoes like huskies pulling dogsleds. Fifty times an hour I'd lunge against a makeshift harness, jerry-rigged from climbing rope and knotted around my chest. The canoe screeched through black spruce trees and lichen-covered boulders. I'd take three steps on firm ground and then stumble into a gaping pit camouflaged with bearberry and alpine azalea, facedown in the Labrador taiga, run over by my own boat. Sucking in blackflies, scratched and bleeding and sweating from places that we didn't know had pores, we dragged ourselves to our feet so we could drag the boat a few feet more.

That doesn't sound very much like fun, huh?

But the payoff was huge. At the bottom of the Rocky Tangle, we paddled through a flat plain, the scenery an unbroken curtain of spruce and tamarack, blueberries, and Labrador tea. Soon the horizon rose up in high, rocky barrens. We crossed lakes in beastly winds, whitecaps slopping over the sides of the canoes, then ground out in bony streambeds, where the water dribbled through hundreds of yards of boulder and cobble. Sometimes we pulled the boats as much as we paddled them, but there wasn't much point to fretting over what might be around the next bend. Nobody knew, and whatever it was, we'd have to make it through as best we could. We were a hundred miles from the nearest road.

One morning we were out of the tents as a rising sun sent plumes of steam boiling off the ice-slicked canoes. Holding plates of grits and bacon, we huddled over topographic maps. They were dog-eared and smeared with ink, but they had come to life, paddle stroke by paddle stroke. By now we knew what an inch of open blue water on the maps looks like in a headwind and how the squiggly contour lines came together to mark mossy rock cliffs crowding our route.

Figuring out the lake crossings took the most headscratching. Turning the maps to line up with the compass, we figured out the far shoreline of the new morning's puzzler. We could see it on the map: Somewhere along a distant smudge of green, our route poured through a twenty-yard-wide outlet and into a narrow gorge. Talk about a needle in a haystack. Miss it by just a few compass degrees, and we could plunge blindly into any number of look-alike box-canyon coves.

We took a reading and pushed off. Forty-five minutes later, we made landfall on a rocky shoreline. A solid wall of woods blocked our passage, with no outfall in sight. We pulled out the maps and compass, wondering where we'd gone wrong.

"Every lake up here looks like an ink blot," I muttered. "We're on a river and there are still eighty-six wrong ways to turn!" We split up to scout the shoreline in opposite directions. Five minutes later Bill Mulvey and David Falkowski whistled and waved paddles, signaling a find. A small, unmarked island had risen from the lake bottom during low water. Behind it lay a tiny outfall that carried the flow of the entire watershed. We could have lost half a day searching for such a small spigot. Our luck, so far, was holding.

By noon low clouds spit cold rain as we dropped out of the last set of rapids in the Kanairiktok's headwaters. Rocky bluffs now pinched the waterway into a true, flowing river, its serpentine route snaking into the distance. The tough business of route-finding was behind us.

That night we collapsed on the rocky shore of an unnamed lake and watched northern lights arc overhead like a lava lamp stretched across the sky. Mars was up, and Bill thought he heard wolves howling. Scott and David stuck their heads out of the tent door to catch the sound, but I crawled to my sleeping bag. I was beat—and we had four more days on the river.

Those are all big stories, some of them big-fish stories, from some of the wildest places left in North America. But the honest truth is you don't have to half drown in places like Alaska and Canada to have crazy canoeing adventures. Here's the deal: I'd bet that within an hour's drive of just about every kid in America, there's a creek or stream or small river that hardly ever sees a canoe. You can spot them on any road map: squiggly little blue lines that run through farm fields and woods. That's what you look for—a few miles of stream between a couple of bridges. Pack fishing rods and bug spray. A big lunch. Better bring a saw or hatchet, just in case you have to hack your way through a blowdown or two.

There's a stream just like this near my home. It uncoils like a wild grapevine through the hardwood bottoms of eastern North Carolina. My first trip down it was unforgettable. When my buddy Sam Toler and I pulled off the side of the road a hundred yards from the bridge, Sam ran down to the water and hooted up through the brambles: "Goo-ooo-oood-ness, the creek is low-low-low. I don't know who I feel sorrier for—us or all those fish we're getting ready to catch."

We carried the canoe through a forty-yard stretch of

brush, littered with a soggy sofa, busted glass, and a couple hundred pounds of old roofing shingles. At the water's edge, cinder blocks, bottles, and Y-shaped fishing-rod sticks suggested we weren't the first ones to drown a cricket in the creek. No big deal. "You know what'll happen," Sam said. "Soon as the bridge is out of sight we'll be in another world."

Ten paddle strokes later, and Sam was right: Tall river birch, gum, and swamp chestnut oaks stretched their branches out to form a canopy overhead. Cypress stumps and cypress knees lined the creek bank. The creek went from fifteen to fifty feet wide and back again—and again, and again. Snakes dripped from the trees with splashes while painted turtles and yellow-belly sliders plopped off. When we were just a football field away from the bridge, the only signs of human presence were jet trails in the sky overhead.

Of course, we weren't on this little creek just for the scenery. We wanted to catch fish, but fishing that water required commando-style casting tactics. I took two paddle strokes, grabbed the rod, and flicked a spinner into undercut banks, then into the deep water on the far side of sandbars, and then smack-dab between big, gray cypress trunks. Backhand, forehand, underhand—most times there was only time for a cast or two before I had to grab a paddle. And most times I was well rewarded. I made a cast: a redbreast sunfish. Another cast: another redbreast. Next a small bass with a large attitude smacked a spinner so hard that lure and fish came out of the water together. He tail-walked halfway to the boat. Just downstream Sam's rod bent over with a two-pound chain pickerel—what locals call a jack. It's essentially a Southern-grown version of a northern pike, small but with a similarly scaled wallop—and teeth.

The fish are willing, but there's a price to be paid on small streams—wading in dank muck, sharing a fifteen-foot-wide body of water with spiders beyond counting and four-foot-long snakes. One time I felt something crawling up my thigh and glanced down at three arachnids of varying species and ranging in diameter from dime-size to I'm-trying-not-to-think-about-it. I smashed the nastiest-looking spider with my elbow in the same movement I use to flick another like a backhanded cast.

Paddle these little creeks and you have to be willing to run like a fullback straight into the nasty stuff. Turning one corner in the creek, we saw that a giant oak tree had fallen across the river, its monstrous crown wedged into the creek bank.

We looked for a way around, or through, the blockage.

"What do you think?" Sam asked. "Far right, maybe?" But he'd already made up his mind, for I could hear him in the stern of the canoe shoving gear out of the way. "Looks like a little hole beside that broken limb," he said. "You ready?"

I grinned and nodded, tucked the rod tips under the gunwales, folded my seat down, and turned my hat backward. "Full speed ahead," I hollered as we dug the paddles hard. Ten seconds later we crashed into the treetop like a train off its tracks. A jagged limb ripped my shirt, drawing blood. A half dozen spiders rained down my back, their webs a wet slime across my sweaty face. A handful of turtles and at least one snake hit the water. Then the canoe suddenly screeched to a halt, held tight in the crotch of a tree.

"Snap, crackle, pop," Sam hooted. "This is my kind of canoeing! Hey, you use the machete. I've got a bow saw around here, somewhere. That wasn't bad at all, was it?"

Not bad at all. At times we paddled for a half hour or more with our feet in the boat. Other times we were in and out time after time in a twenty-minute stretch, hauling the canoe over or around moss-slicked logs, squirming hand-over-hand spelunker-style under poison-ivy-meshed trunks, and slashing our way through treetops by means of various edged weapons.

But man, the fishing! When we heard a truck rumble across a bridge, we knew we were close to the takeout. We tallied up the score: In seven miles of stream, we'd been forced to haul the canoe over logjams and blowdowns twenty times. We'd broken one rod in a crash-dive through a treetop, and I must have smashed at least thirty spiders into my arms, legs, belly, and noggin. We'd not seen a human footprint or a piece of trash. Along the way we'd landed 175 redbreast sunfish, fifteen largemouth bass, a dozen bluegill, three jacks, and a pair of suckers. And I would be home in time for supper.

Maybe that crooked little close-to-home river wasn't as big and wild as Alaska's Kipchuk or Labrador's Kanairiktok. But the memories were just as large. And if there's one thing I've learned from a lifetime of canoeing wild waters, it's this: Every bend in every river is a door to a stretch of brand-new water that you're paddling for the very first time. It's hard to beat that kind of adventure.

ABOUT
GUYS READ

It's true: Guys Read true stories. And you just proved it. (Unless you just opened the book to this page and started reading. In which case, we feel bad for you because you missed some pretty awesome stuff.)

Now what?

Now we keep going—Guys Read keeps working to find good stuff for you to read, you read it and pass it along to other guys. Here's how we can do it:

For more than ten years, Guys Read has been at www.guysread.com, collecting recommendations of what guys really want to read. We have gathered recommendations of thousands of great funny books, scary books, action books, illustrated books, information books, wordless books, sci-fi books, mystery books, and you-name-it books.

So what's your part of the job? Simple: try out some of the suggestions at guysread.com, try some of the other stuff written by the authors in this book, and then let us know what you think. Tell us what you like to read. Tell us what you don't like to read. The more you tell us, the more great book recommendations we can collect. It might even help us choose the writers for the next installment of Guys Read.

Thanks for reading.

And thanks for helping Guys Read.

JON SCIESZKA (editor) has been writing books for children ever since he took time off from his career as an elementary school teacher. He wanted to create funny books that kids would want to read. Once he got going, he never stopped. He is the author of numerous picture books, middle grade series, and even a memoir. From 2007–2010 he served as the first National Ambassador for Children's Literature, appointed by the Library of Congress. Since 2004, Jon has been actively promoting his interest in getting boys to read through his Guys Read initiative and website. Born in Flint, Michigan, Jon now lives in Brooklyn with his family. Visit him online at www.jsworldwide.com and at www.guysread.com.

SELECTED TITLES

THE TRUE STORY OF THE THREE LITTLE PIGS
(Illustrated by Lane Smith)

THE STINKY CHEESE MAN
AND OTHER FAIRLY STUPID TALES
(Illustrated by Lane Smith)

The Time Warp Trio series, including SUMMER READING
IS KILLING ME (Illustrated by Lane Smith)

The Spaceheadz series

CANDACE FLEMING ("A Jumbo Story") found her calling as a storyteller very early in life. As a preschooler, she told her neighbors about Spot, her three-legged cat. Her kindergarten classmates heard about the ghost that lived in her attic. In first grade she told her teacher about her family's trip to Paris, France. Everyone thought she was telling the truth. She wasn't. She just liked telling a good story . . . and watching for the reaction. Today Candy likes telling true stories just as much as the ones she makes up. She has written many award-winning books, both fiction and nonfiction, usually incorporating what she loves most: stories, musical language, and history. Visit her online at www.candacefleming.com.

SELECTED TITLES

AMELIA LOST:
The Life and Disappearance of Amelia Earhart

THE GREAT AND ONLY BARNUM:
*The Tremendous, Stupendous Life of
Showman P. T. Barnum*

BEN FRANKLIN'S ALMANAC:
Being A True Account of the Good Gentleman's Life

THE LINCOLNS:
A Scrapbook Look at Abraham and Mary

BRIAN FLOCA (Illustrator) grew up in Temple, Texas. He credits his interest in gears and machinery at least partly to childhood visits to the family business, a soft-drink bottling plant. He has always loved drawing and cartooning, and created a daily comic strip in his college newspaper. He illustrated his first book, the graphic novel CITY OF LIGHT, CITY OF DARK by Avi, shortly after graduating. He enjoys illustrating books by other authors for the way they introduce him to new subjects, stories, and characters, and enjoys writing and illustrating his own books for the chance they give him to explore his own interests. His books have received three Sibert Honors. Visit him online at www.brianfloca.com.

SELECTED TITLES

LOCOMOTIVE

MOONSHOT: *The Flight of Apollo 11*

THE RACECAR ALPHABET

LIGHTSHIP

DOUGLAS FLORIAN ("Uni-verses") grew up in New York City and started his career as a cartoonist for the *New Yorker* magazine. One day he ran across a collection of children's poems that inspired him to start writing poems and creating illustrations to go along with them, often using paper bags as his canvas. "Poetry," he says, "is not black-and-white. It is more like the gray-and-purple area that connects all the things we live in." He likes to write poems about stuff that especially interests him, like trees, lizards, frogs, cats, dogs, honeybees, pirates, baseballs, space, and dinosaurs. Visit him online at www.douglasflorianbooks.com.

SELECTED TITLES

POEM RUNS: *Baseball Poems*

UNBEELIEVABLES:
Honeybee Poems and Paintings

COMETS, STARS, THE MOON, AND MARS:
Space Poems and Paintings

DINOTHESAURUS: *Prehistoric Poems and Paintings*

NATHAN HALE ("Hugh Glass: Dead Man Crawling") is not sure if he is related to the Revolutionary War spy Nathan Hale, but he knows he is not a direct descendant because the famous spy was killed before he had any children. Nathan did not start getting interested in comic books until he was in high school (because up until then he spent nearly all his time playing video games). When he did get into comics, he illustrated the Eisner-nominated graphic novel *Rapunzel's Revenge*. Besides his work as an illustrator, he has painted scientific murals for museums around the United States. He also collects LEGO sets and runs marathons—seven so far (marathons, not LEGO sets). Visit him online at www.spacestationnathan.com.

SELECTED TITLES

Nathan Hale's Hazardous Tales series,
including TREATIES, TRENCHES, MUD, AND BLOOD,
and DONNER DINNER PARTY

THANHHA LAI ("A Pack of Brothers") was born in Vietnam in 1965 (The Year of the Snake), the youngest of nine children. Life was good—she went to school, ate lots of snacks, and was "top dog" in her class. When the war ended on April 30, 1975, she and her family scrambled onto a navy ship and ended up in Montgomery, Alabama. It took Thanhha and her family about ten years to get used to life in the United States. By then they lived in Texas, where Thanhha studied journalism in college. She worked as a newspaper reporter and then began to write fiction. Her novel in verse INSIDE OUT & BACK AGAIN won the National Book Award and was a Newbery Honor Book. She lives north of New York City.

SELECTED TITLE

INSIDE OUT & BACK AGAIN

SY MONTGOMERY ("Tarantula Heaven") has been chased by an angry silverback gorilla in Zaire, has been bitten by a vampire bat in Costa Rica, has worked in a pit crawling with 18,000 snakes in Manitoba, and has handled a wild tarantula in French Guiana in the course of researching her books. She has also been deftly undressed by an orangutan in Borneo, has been hunted by a tiger in India, and has swum with piranhas, electric eels, and dolphins in the Amazon. An ardent conservationist, she is a board member of Restore: The North Woods and the Center for Tropical Conservation. Visit her online at www.symontgomery.com.

JIM MURPHY ("This Won't Hurt a Bit: The Painfully True Story of Dental Care") is a two-time Newbery Honor Book and Sibert Award–winning author. He also received the Margaret A. Edwards Award for significant contribution to young adult literature. Growing up, he didn't care much about reading until a teacher named a book the students were absolutely forbidden to read. Jim rushed to read the forbidden book and then kept on reading—anything he could get his hands on. He was also a high school track star—and was a member of two national champion relay teams at the Penn Relays. Visit him online at www.jimmurphybooks.com.

T. EDWARD NICKENS ("The River's Run") is editor-at-large for *Field & Stream* magazine and a contributing editor for *Audubon* magazine. He writes about outdoor sports, natural history, and conservation. He's reported from the Arctic to Central America, on topics as varied as Cajun culture and jaguar conservation, winning more than two dozen national writing awards. He writes, produces, and hosts television and webisode features on locations across North America. You can find videos and more of his stories at www.fieldandstream.com.

SELECTED TITLE

THE TOTAL OUTDOORSMAN MANUAL: *374 Skills You Need*

ELIZABETH PARTRIDGE ("Mojo, Moonshine, and the Blues") was an acupuncturist for more than twenty years before becoming a full-time writer. She grew up in a family of photographers—including her grandmother Imogen Cunningham, and her godmother, Dorothea Lange. She is inspired by the artists she has been surrounded by her whole life and hopes the stories she writes about creative and amazing people are inspiring to her readers. She says, "I hope they will ignite the creative, brave, idealistic energy young adults have, and let them know: they too can make a difference in our crazy, turbulent world." Visit her online at www.elizabethpartridge.com.

SELECTED TITLES

MARCHING FOR FREEDOM: *Walk Together Children and Don't You Grow Weary*

JOHN LENNON: *All I Want Is the Truth*

THIS LAND WAS MADE FOR YOU AND ME: *The Life and Songs of Woody Guthrie*

DOROTHEA LANGE: *Grab a Hunk of Lightning*

STEVE SHEINKIN ("Sahara Shipwreck") was born in Brooklyn, New York, and lived in Mississippi and Colorado before settling in the suburbs north of New York City. As a kid, his favorite books were action stories and outdoor adventures, stuff like sea stories, searches for buried treasure, and sharks eating people. His all-time favorite book is *Mutiny on the Bounty,* a novel based on the true story of a famous mutiny aboard a British ship in the late 1700s. He also loves to read anything about baseball, and still has his baseball card collection, in case you want to do a little trading. He has received the Sibert Medal, the YALSA Award for Excellence in Nonfiction, and a Newbery Honor. He was also a National Book Award finalist. Visit him online at www.stevesheinkin.com.

SELECTED TITLES

BOMB: *The Race to Build—and Steal—the World's Most Dangerous Weapon*

THE PORT CHICAGO 50: *Disaster, Mutiny, and the Fight For Civil Rights*

LINCOLN'S GRAVE ROBBERS

THE NOTORIOUS BENEDICT ARNOLD: *A True Story of Adventure, Heroism & Treachery*

JAMES STURM ("A Cartoonist's Course") loves comics so much he helped start a cartooning school, The Center for Cartoon Studies, in White River Junction, Vermont. Many of James's graphic novels are about American history, including SATCHEL PAIGE: *Striking Out Jim Crow* and JAMES STURM'S AMERICA: *God, Gold, and Golems*. Even UNSTABLE MOLECULES, the comic featuring his favorite childhood superheroes, the Fantastic Four, was about American history! James is also the cocreator of the popular Adventures in Cartooning series that offers inspiration and instruction for kids who want to make their own comics.

SELECTED TITLES

ADVENTURES IN CARTOONING:
How to Turn Your Doodles into Comics

ADVENTURES IN CARTOONING: *Characters in Action*

MARKET DAY

Jon Scieszka presents
THE GUYS READ LIBRARY
OF GREAT READING

Volume 1

Volume 2

Volume 3

Volume 4

Volume 5

Read them all!

WALDEN POND PRESS™
An Imprint of HarperCollinsPublishers

www.harpercollinschildrens.com
www.walden.com/books